MECH FORCE: HELLFIRE

RICK PARTLOW

DREW AVERA

HELLFIRE
©2019-2022 RICK PARTLOW
& DREW AVERA

This book is protected under the copyright laws of the United States of America. No part of this publication may be reproduced, stored in a retrieval system, or transmitted, in any form or by any means, without the prior permission in writing of the publisher, nor be otherwise circulated in any form of binding or cover other than that in which it is published and without a similar condition including this condition being imposed on the subsequent purchaser. Any reproduction or unauthorized use of the material or artwork contained herein is prohibited without the express written permission of the authors.

Aethon Books supports the right to free expression and the value of copyright. The purpose of copyright is to encourage writers and artists to produce the creative works that enrich our culture.

The scanning, uploading, and distribution of this book without permission is a theft of the author's intellectual property. If you would like to use material from the book (other than for review purposes), please contact editor@aethonbooks.com. Thank you for your support of the author's rights.

Aethon Books
www.aethonbooks.com

Print and eBook formatting, and cover design by Steve Beaulieu. Published by Aethon Books LLC.

Aethon Books is not responsible for websites (or their content) that are not owned by the publisher.

This book is a work of fiction. Names, characters, places, and incidents are the product of the author's imagination or are used fictitiously. Any resemblance to actual events, locales, or persons, living or dead is coincidental.

All rights reserved.

ALSO IN THE SERIES_

HELLFIRE
BRIMSTONE
APOCALYPSE

PROLOGUE_

Pain speared through my forehead like a needle of plasma straight from the heart of a star and I sat up in bed, crying out. The shout died aborning, drowned out by the alarm klaxons, and I was sure for just a brief, waking moment that the warbling scream was inside my head, an illusion brought on by the fiery agony.

But the pain faded into the background and the klaxons remained and I slapped the touchpad for the lights, half expecting to see my barracks room in flames and collapsing around me. Instead, my "I love me" wall stared back at me in a series of certificates declaring Captain Nathaniel Stout was good-to-go, high-speed and ripe for promotion as far as the United States Army was concerned. Below the certificates and diplomas was something even more important to me: a small, framed photo of a compact, wiry dark-haired man in an olive-drab flight suit---me, unless the image in the mirror had changed while I was sleeping---and a chubbier, taller, slightly older man in work coveralls stained with grease, my best friend, Robert Franklin. Despite being dressed like a construction worker, he was the CEO of Franklin Enterprises and the designer of the machine we stood beside in the picture, my reason for being here.

Is it a drill? I leaned against the bed with my left hand, feet swinging off the side, hesitant to get up for what might be just another circle jerk by the brass to prove how ready we were.

Then the walls shook with the concussion of something far away, but not far *enough* away for me to ignore it.

Sonic boom? I thought hopefully.

Another crashing explosion, much closer, and my graduation certificate from Army Aviation School pitched forward to the cheap carpeting.

Shit.

I was out of bed before the sound of cracking glass registered in my brain. I grabbed my flight suit out of the open closet, not understanding why no one had come looking for me. If this was an attack, why the hell wouldn't they call me, or knock on my door?

Unless they're too busy being dead.

The flight suit went on with rote motions, my hands working from memories too deep to be affected by the haze over everything else from the lingering migraine.

I didn't used to have migraines, did I? I couldn't remember.

Boots strapped, I grabbed my ID tag and fastened it to a Velcro patch on my arm and hesitated for just a moment at the door. The knob didn't feel hot, so there wasn't a fire outside. The only thing I'd have to worry about was getting shot.

Who would be shooting at me again? Who were we fighting?

It seemed like something I should know, something I should remember. It didn't want to come to me, though, and there wasn't time to stand around and coax it out. Whatever I couldn't remember, I did recall where I should be and what I should be doing. I yanked open the door and ducked through into a hallway filled with smoke.

I threw my arm across my mouth and nose automatically in conditioned reflex, slitting my eyes and running blindly along a route I'd traveled in pitch darkness during blackout drills. The alarm was even louder out here and the pain in my head seemed to intensify with each second of exposure to the unceasing wail. If I hadn't known better, I would have sworn someone was actually digging a red-hot scalpel into my temple, trying to get to the gooey caramel center.

I would have asked someone to look at my head and tell me if I was bleeding or something, but there was no one around. The hallways were deserted and that seemed very wrong. I expected someone to be here, but who? Flight crew? Engineers? Mechanics? Robert?

Swinging plastic doors with a window at eye level on each, but I couldn't see anything through them for the smoke. I crashed through anyway into a broader hallway, offices maybe, workshops. Posters on the wall, unclear through the haze in the air and in my head. Schematics, circuit diagrams, skeletal views of weapons and their mounts. Recruiting posters, some of them defaced with markers, adding improbable endowments to the men and women in them.

I knew where I was, even if I couldn't put a name to it. The hangar was what I wanted and it was straight ahead, through another set of doors, larger ones. So was the source of the smoke, so were the explosions, coming more often now. Mortars, I somehow knew, walking to their target a few dozen meters at a time.

I found the first bodies just this side of the door. I couldn't put a name to them, just faceless drones I'd seen running errands around the base, enlisted under someone else's command who never spoke to me. A man, his skin the color of aged ebony, a few years younger than me, a Spec-4's rank on his collar. His eyes were white and wide and permanently open, his mouth slack, lips stained with blood. He was lying on his chest, head turned to the side, and I couldn't tell what had killed him. It hadn't been smoke inhalation.

The woman off to the side of him was a civilian, dressed in coveralls, clean but with old stains ground in that would never come out, and new, red ones soaking into them. She had a gaping wound in her throat, wide enough I could see the white of her vertebrae through it, drained of blood now. The blood was on the floor, spreading in a puddle a meter across, all the way from her to the dead Specialist.

The doors were still shut, though there was a gaping, blackened, smoking hole through them where the fragments that had killed the two of them had penetrated. I didn't really want to see what was on the other side, but something was screaming inside my head, something behind the pain, maybe *in* the pain, telling me I had a job to do. I hopped over the blood and put a shoulder into the right-hand door, slipping through the gap before it was all the way open.

So, this was where everyone had gone.

The bodies were torn and charred, clothing shredded or burned, grotesque caricatures of humanity. They reminded me of the plastic dummies I'd seen in High School health classes, the skin peeled away to expose the muscles and bones and organs, except there hadn't been the sticky, sickly-sweet stench of blood and burnt flesh in the health classes. The smoke was good. I knew the fires engulfing the other end of the hangar would burn the whole thing down eventually---there seemed to be no one left to fight them---but the smoke was doing its best to hide the bodies from my view, to drown out the sickening smell. The wind from the open hangar doors, from the rends and jagged holes in the walls, was trying to draw it off, pull its concealing blanket away from the carnage; but each time it tried, it fed more oxygen to the blaze and it flared again with a fresh billow of snarling, black haze.

The fires, the smoke, the wrecked sections of hangar had been direct mortar hits on the mechs. Their absence was a cratered, flaming gap in the landscape, and if I couldn't have named even one of the other pilots, I could recite chapter and verse of their technical specs, their fuel capacity, their typical weapons load. One still stood, wreathed in a cloak of grey and black, only meters from the edge of a fire licking at an ammo locker. I ran to it, a lost child racing for the arms of his mother amidst the chaos and panic.

Bob lay at the circular, pad-like feet of the bipedal, metal beast, hand stretched out as if asking her for help in his last moments. Robert Franklin hadn't died as ugly as the others, but death had claimed him still. The blood soaking his coveralls didn't have an obvious source, but bomb fragments from a mortar could be as small as a coil of spring. An emptiness roiled in my gut at the sight of him, but there was something else, something wrong about his face. Maybe it was the slack indignity of death, but he looked so much *older* than he should have, older than the picture in my room, older than I remembered.

I didn't have the time to stand there and stare at him. A rolling chain of explosions thundered in from the edge of the edge of the airstrip, getting closer, nearly drowning out the screaming whine of the jets. The attack wasn't over and if I stayed here, I'd wind up just as dead as Bob. I edged past his body, afraid to touch him, as if he'd developed some dread, communicable disease and I would drop dead at first contact.

I had no such fears of the Hellfire. She waited for me with open arms, and the death she promised wasn't something to be dreaded, but rather embraced. I grabbed at the latch for the cockpit entry hatch, jumping up and snagging it one-handed rather than hunting down the portable stairs and hauling them into place. The clam-shell canopy lowered in silent invitation and I clutched at the handholds, justifying all those pull-ups I did twice a day at the base gym. Another lunge upward, grabbing the seat, cold plastic, hard and unyielding, and wrestling into it, slipping my arm and legs through the safety restraints and buckling them with a comforting series of clicks.

My helmet stared at me darkly through a mirrored visor, hanging from the control harness impatiently, showing the reflected image of my face, pale and drawn and not looking at all well. Tired of its discontented glare and scared of my own visage, I pulled it over my head, plugging the oxygen hose into the connection beside my seat and strapping the mask into place.

The power-up procedure was as ingrained as brushing my teeth. I felt the pressure against the edge of my fingers as I flipped the switches, but it could have been someone else's hands going through the motions. I watched the control board light up as if I were a spectator at a NASCAR race, rooting for the system to finish its cycle. Turbines grumbled low, speeding up into a scream, a savage battle cry, begging to be set free of her restraints and leap into the contest.

"Yeah, let's do that."

There were a series of diagnostic checks demanding to be run, but I bypassed them, earning a scolding from the computer systems. I ignored it and pushed the turbines into the red, feeding them air and fuel and setting them loose. The textbook takeoff procedure for the Hellfire Pi-Mech was a slow buildup to a hover, then a nice, steady cruise to operational altitude. I got in trouble with Bob constantly for goosing her right out of the hangar, but I think even he would have given me his blessing under the circumstances.

Acceleration shoved me back into hard plastic, every millimeter of its surface impressed into my torso through the flight suit, and I wished Bob had listened to me about adding some sort of cushion to it, and the weight penalty be damned.

When did I tell him that? Was that yesterday? A year ago?

The hangar disappeared and my doubts with it. Radar and lidar and thermal sensors chirped in annoying chorus for attention, but I didn't need their help. I could see the threats very well, thanks so much, even if I couldn't quite believe them. I'd expected helicopters, maybe drones, some armored infantry. What I got was mechs.

Nothing as sophisticated as the Hellfire, of course, but still mechs, manned and unmanned, squat, bipedal shapes silhouetted against the gold-red ball of the rising sun.

Why had I slept in? What had happened yesterday? Why couldn't I remember yesterday?

Three of them still patrolled the sky a hundred meters or so off the ground, a manned Pi-mech and two U-mechs, drones, their jets spilling out heat mirages in their wake, firing at some threat on the ground every few seconds with precision bursts from their cannon. Another two had already landed, loping forward across the airstrip on ostrich-bent legs, their gait ridiculous and yet ridiculously fast.

More mysteries—I'd expected them to be Russian Tagans. Who else would be attacking us? But these were domestic designs, unmarked, unflagged. Mercenaries. Sent by who?

Or is that whom?

I shrugged. I couldn't decide, so I launched a missile. I would have launched more, but I only had four of them and had to be choosy. The Xyston kicked free on a puff of inert gas before the main rocket motor ignited and it flared away from my left shoulder, taking only two seconds to cover the kilometer between my Hellfire and the enemy Cobra hovering between the two U-mechs. You could tell the manned version by the control dish mounted above the cockpit, like the old whip antennae on the RTO in infantry units of decades past, making him a high-value target.

He hadn't seen my launch, hadn't expected any opposition and he wasn't ready for it. His automated CWIS spun the Vulcan on his right shoulder toward the incoming missile, but I was too close and there was no hope. The Xyston anti-armor missile took him in the portside turbine and ripped his mech apart in mid-air, sending one of the twin turbines sailing kilometers away on a track of black smoke and engulfing what was left in ravaging fire. He fell out of the air with a sickening inevitability, tumbling and rolling and I hoped for his sake he was already dead, because impact wasn't the way I wanted to go.

The U-mechs continued to hover, motionless, waiting for a command signal that wasn't going to come, and I took the opportunity to rake them with cannon fire. The 40mm rounds tore through their jet turbines and gravity took care of the rest, sending them to join their control mech. Miniature mushroom clouds marked their crashes, but I wasn't waiting around to watch their denouement. I was heading down again, spiraling around behind the twin Cobras already on the ground, the old welcome flip-flop feeling hitting my stomach with the descent. I'd use to get it when I flew Comanche scout choppers, but this was as close as I got anymore.

Wait. When had I flown Comanches? How long ago was that?

They'd seen me. It was too much to hope they wouldn't notice. I'd gotten lucky with the ones in the air, and luck didn't last. Nothing ever lasted.

They were shooting at me. I saw the missiles leave their launch racks, not state-of-the-art Xystons, but much older Javelins, probably picked up on the black market for cheap. Easy to spoof, easy to jam. Why were they even wasting their time? My Hellfire touched tarmac, her legs bending backward digitigrade as the hips absorbed the landing, but the missiles kept going, spiraling upward, unguided, ignored.

The cockpit was a video arcade from the movies my father used to watch, lights flashing, warnings beeping for attention, alerting me to radar and lidar scans, missile locks and enemy detected and hell, that my breakfast was ready and I'd left my keys in my car for all I knew. It was background noise—I knew what was coming and where it was coming from, and I was already giving it back.

One more missile, the flare of its launch a star in my vision, the white clouds of its exhaust curling around my cockpit, obscuring my sightlines. I didn't need them. Radar and lidar and thermal and sonic sensors painted a computer-simulated tactical portrait in the targeting reticle of my helmet, showing me the two Cobras turning toward my Hellfire, white fire flashing from the .50-cal rotary cannons they mounted at the end of their left arms.

Something wrenched hard against the right side of my Hellfire, armor-piercing 750-grain .50 caliber Browning Machine Gun bullets shattering part of the plastron on my mech's right chest, not quite penetrating to the vitals beneath but coming too damned close. Not bad for a round designed 150 years ago, but I preferred a slightly more modern weapon. My targeting reticle lit up a solid green on the Cobra to my right. I ignored the one on the left because he was the center of a swiftly-expanding ball of white, yellow and red fire and pieces of him were showering down on the tarmac. God, I love Xystons, and no one has figured out a way to jam them yet. I squeezed the trigger on the right-hand control stick of the Hellfire's steering yoke and the 20mm Vulcan that took up most of her right arm cleared its throat, coughing up ten, massive, tungsten slugs.

Sparks showered from the Cobra's left arm and shoulder, honeycomb boron armor shattering and splintering from the first two or three slugs before the ones coming in fractions of a second later chewed through the muscle fibers and servomotors and took the shoulder joint off in a cloud of electrical fireflies from severed power cables. The Cobra stumbled off to the side, its balance thrown off by the sudden loss of an arm laden down with a tri-barrel .50-cal cannon and thousands of rounds of ammo for it.

I didn't give him a chance to recover and I didn't stand there like a dumbass either. In any gunfight, whether you're on foot, in a chopper or in a mech, movement is life. I jogged to my left, circling around, keeping the Hellfire's upper body twisted toward the crippled enemy, not giving him a chance to line up the twin forties mounted to his right shoulder. I fired the Vulcan again, another ten-round burst, and turned his right-side turbine into scrap, the cylindrical pod exploding as the vanes came apart at speed.

That was it for him. I didn't finish him off, because there wasn't a need to and because mech pilots, no matter who they fought for, shared something of a code. You didn't fire on a helpless mech and you didn't kill the pilot if he got out, because someday, that could be you in there. The damned Russians didn't always go by the code, but I did because of something about the Golden Rule and karma and shit.

No more targets on the airstrip, but there had to be more. Five mechs hadn't taken down the whole base. I was sure there was infantry coming in somewhere, probably up the front approaches. A few running steps and a stomp on the throttle and the Hellfire was back in the sky, rising on columns of superheated air. I rose through the clouds of dark smoke billowing over the hangar, cruising at thirty meters up over the boring, warehouse-basic roof of the complex.

Out beyond the airstrip and the parking lots, I could see the high desert, bleeding red with the sunrise, and the snow-capped mountains in the distance. They seemed clean and untouched and I envied them. Back on the ground, things were a lot dirtier. Smaller columns of smoke were adding their output to the dark smudge rising over the base and...

What was the name of the place? Why the hell couldn't I remember the name?

There they were. Infantry in armored personnel carriers, some of the vehicles already burning, skidded aside from the main gate under fire from the guard posts. The turrets at the gate were silent now, contributors to the smoke. The men and women who'd been stationed out there might have fallen back to cover inside the buildings. Maybe they get away. I told myself that, hoping they were taking off across the desert, getting out of this alive.

Heads went up among the troopers streaming through the front gate, brown camouflage doing its best to blend in with the background but not quite making it. They'd seen me and they were firing their rifles, 6.5mm anti-personnel rounds at two hundred meters. Even if they hit me, the bullets were spitballs against the Hellfire's armor. Still, best not to encourage bad behavior.

I switched the 40mm cannons to anti-personnel rounds and fired a spread into the middle of the troops. The recoil pushed the Hellfire back in its hover and I had to open the throttle a bit more to compensate, but the results were worth the effort. Black blossoms of smoke marked detonations, a line of them springing up across the front parking lot, running from the back bumper of a beat-up Toyota to the front windshield of one of the busses they used to ferry people in from the park-and-ride. Enemy troops littered the space between, tossed to the ground by the blasts, some writhing in agony, some not moving at all.

I brought the Hellfire down in the middle of the access road running from the front entrance out to the airstrip, breaking into a long, loping run, the footpads of the Hellfire cracking the pavement where they struck. I could do this. If this was everything they'd brought, I could take enough of them out that they'd have to retreat. Then I'd call in support and we could secure the place until...

Until what? What support? Who the hell ran this place?

I had a sudden urge to just take off, fly toward those mountains until my fuel ran out, then abandon the Hellfire and just walk. No one would know. I could go find Cecelia and...

Find her where? Where was I?

Infantry interrupted the questions, rushing forward around the corner of the building, rifles firing like ineffectual mosquitoes. The 20mm would have been a waste, so I used the coaxial machine guns, raking them with a few hundred rounds of 6.5mm and sending them scurrying away.

Damned crunchies.

I didn't notice the MANPAD until it was too late. One of those annoying flashes I could almost ignore, and the whining tone of a laser designator being detected and I was looking everywhere for another mech or a chopper or one of the APCs until I saw the missile team right at the corner of the facility where the road curved. I was clutching the trigger of the machine guns when they fired. There were only a couple hundred meters separating us and the missile arrived before I could even think of deploying countermeasures and I did the only thing I could think of and jammed my heels down on the pedals and jumped the Hellfire into the air.

I don't know how high I was when the missile hit, but it was high enough to eject. I didn't make the choice myself, Hellfire's fail-safes did it for me in far less time than a human could have. I don't know if the massive concussive blast was from the missile striking the turbines or the ejection rockets carrying the cockpit pod clear of the main body of the mech, but it hurt like a son of a bitch either way.

I saw nothing but light and fire, heard nothing but thunder, felt nothing but pain. I was falling, and I was burning...and then everything was darkness.

CHAPTER ONE_

Nate Stout sucked in a lungful of cancer and reflected, not for the first time, that Norfolk was a shithole.

It wasn't just the crumbling remains of the Naval base, or the acres of charred ruins left from the terrorist nuke that had taken out the downtown area five years ago. It was a literal shithole. Chesapeake Bay smelled of human refuse, dumped with impunity by the remnant population, unchecked by government oversight because there was no government left. The water was brown and green and just about every color but blue, and after all this time, dead fish and sea birds still floated, rotting, adding their stench to the general miasma.

Wonder how many diseases I'm exposing myself to just breathing this shit? Nate mused.

Enough he didn't even care about the lack of filters in the black-market Russian cigarettes. He let his lungs burn with the smoke for three full seconds before he let it waft out his nostrils with a pleasant burning sensation.

"Aren't you worried about cancer?" Roach asked him.

He tossed the glowing butt at the rusted hulk of what had once been a destroyer and turned away from bad memories, some of which weren't even his own. Rachel Mata, "Roach," was young and looked it, unlike him. She stood watching him, flight suit unzipped and pulled down to her waist, baring her sleeveless T-shirt to the miserable afternoon heat. Her hands were on her hips and she had the sort of look of affectionate disapproval you'd expect from a younger sister. If he'd had a younger sister.

Maybe I did. Who the fuck knows?

He only had the memories Bob Franklin had deemed useful.

"No," Nate answered her. "I'm worried about the mission. Is Dix ready?"

"He sent me to get you. He said, and I quote, 'tell our distinguished commander to get his ass into a mech unless he wants me to lead the damned op.'"

"Oh, I'm so tempted to take him up on that." He winced at the persistent ache in his knees as he followed her back up the pier and into the old military warehouse.

Faded sheet metal, scarred by fire and defaced by generations of graffiti, baked in the sun, and Broken Arrow Mercenary Force simmered inside. He'd winced when Dix had suggested the name, winced even harder when Roach had insisted they all get matching tattoos. She wore hers proudly, on her left forearm, while his was concealed on his right shoulder, invisible usually, though at the moment he had his flight suit unzipped and his T-shirt sleeves rolled up against the summer heat and the red arrow with BAMF superimposed across it was on display.

Suns out, guns out, they'd used to say. Back then, they meant something different.

Nate's fingers brushed the barrel shrouds of his Hellfire's 20mm Vulcan rotary cannon as he passed beneath the machine, threading his way through the underbrush of ammo cans, generators and fire extinguishers and into the midst of the rest of his team.

"Officer on deck!" Brian Richardson barked, coming to attention in front of his own mech, a Hellfire identical to Nate's except for slightly different armament.

Dix had the face to match the tone, hard and lined and marked by experience and responsibility, eyes as blue as a mountain stream off a glacier and just as cold. He couldn't hold it though, and his stiff, serious expression broke down into a snort of amusement. The others laughed outright, younger and impressionable.

"Sorry, Cap," Dix said, punching him lightly on the arm. "I know you were Army, so you don't know what a 'deck' is. Or soap, or a toothbrush..."

"Hey Ramirez," Nate said, nodding to the baby of the group. At twenty-one, he was younger even than Roach, and he hung over every word of "real" veterans like Dix or Nate. "You know how the Navy separates the men from the boys?"

"No, sir," Ramirez shook his head. He wore a buzz cut because he thought it made him look more military, but he'd let a cheesy mustache creep across his lip the last two weeks.

"With a crowbar."

Snorts and chuckles at the old punchline, but more at the tradition of it. BAMF didn't run an op without Army-Navy jokes. He missed the Air Force. Air Force jokes had been the easiest, but fighter jets were fucking expensive and worse than useless in the war they were fighting, and the Chair Force had gone the way of the dodo.

"You got those damned u-mechs working, finally, Dix?" he asked, turning serious. He motioned at the line of remotely-piloted Cobras against the far wall. Theoretically, they could be slaved to the controls of the Hellfire pi-mechs to mirror their targeting and maneuvering, but in practice...

"Finally, boss," Dix hissed out a sigh, facing the beaten and battered machines with a look of utter disgust. "The damned things are older than you and getting their control systems to synch up with the new hardware on our Hellfires has been a royal pain in the ass. I think they'll work now, though."

"You *think*?" Patterson repeated, eyes wide as he stepped out of their makeshift bathroom, separated from the rest of the warehouse by a shower curtain. "Jesus, Dix!" His voice got louder the closer he approached them, wiping his hands dry on his T-shirt. "We're about to wave our happy asses in the wind, I'd kind of like it if you knew!"

Nate cocked an eyebrow at the big man. Patty was what everyone called him after a dare in Tijuana involving a dress and a bad-tempered chihuahua, but Nate always found Geoff Patterson something of a cipher whatever you called him, more difficult to read than Dix or the two youngsters. Patty was tall and gangly, with blond hair so far past regulation that he tied it into a pony tail, and he had a Kentucky accent thick enough to cut with a fork. How the hell he'd wound up here was a question he'd never been willing to answer except with the obvious response: "for the money." He was just this side of thirty, but what he'd done with his youth he wouldn't say, either.

"If Dix says they're working," he told Patty, putting a bit of a reproving edge into his voice, "then they're working. Unless you've suddenly become a better mechanic than I remember, in which case, I will be happy to put you to work."

"Naw, man," Patty said, raising a hand in surrender. "If you're happy with it, it's cool. Just life or death, you know? Nothing serious."

"All right, this is standard procedure," Nate said, slipping out of pre-mission banter and into his professional, business face. "We're going out in teams of two, each slaved to a U-mech. Patty, you're going to hang back at a central point between our patrol areas and act as our reserve. Any of us gets into shit too deep to wade through, you come roaring to the rescue like the cavalry, got it?"

"What's the objective?" Roach asked. "What are the Russians after, and why here?"

"The spooks don't know," Nate admitted, leaning heavily against the leg of his Hellfire. His knees were killing him, but he forced his face into careful neutrality. You could bullshit with the troops, but you couldn't show them weakness. "They don't know much…"

"What else is new?" Patty murmured, arms crossed over his chest.

"At ease with that shit," Dix growled. "Use your ears, not your mouth."

The younger man glowered at him, but said nothing, and Nate went on.

"All the Intell geeks could say was that the Russians have a military presence here at the port and the best guess is, they're trying to smuggle something in past the coastal blockades. A weapon, most likely. Maybe nuclear, maybe biological."

"Who'd notice another nuke in this dump?" Patty again, said so softly Nate barely made it out, but it still earned a dirty look from Dix.

"It wouldn't be used here," Nate explained anyway, not showing the impatience he felt. "They'd probably be trying to take it overland to one of the remaining East Coast enclaves, trying to destabilize the remaining government centers."

"If you don't want your Goddamned kids growing up speaking Russian," Dix said in a quarterdeck bellow he'd picked up from a CAG somewhere back when he'd been a pilot, "then maybe you should take this shit seriously." He waved at the map someone had taped to the wall to cover a cluster of bullet holes. It was an older map of the US, without the depressing additions and subtractions of the last ten years. "If you ever want America to look like *that* again, we need to do our fucking jobs!"

"Ooh-rah, Lt. Richardson," Patty offered half-heartedly. "Point me at a Marine recruiter." The tall man chuckled. "Oh, right, there ain't none anymore. Now it's the 'Combined Coastal Defense,' or some shit like that. We ain't got an Air Force, we ain't got a Navy, we ain't got the Marines and the Army just throws money at guys like us to do their work for them. You seriously think *that*..." He shot a bird at the map. "...is ever coming back?"

"Something bothering you, Patterson?" Nate asked him instead of kicking his ass and spitting on the remains, which was what he sorely wanted to do.

"No, boss," he answered too quickly, waving it off. "I'm up for it, I guess I'm just not in a rah-rah mood today." He jerked a thumb at his Hellfire. "Is there anything more to the briefing or can I start firing up Matilda?"

"Naw, go ahead. We move out in five mikes. Everyone gear up, get strapped in and check the slave circuits for the U-mechs."

As the others moved off, Nate bent down, leaning his butt against the right leg of his Hellfire to support him as he fastened the straps of his combat boots. His legs and back let him know exactly what they thought of the maneuver and he sucked in a breath as he straightened up.

Wonder if I have time to pop some ibuprofen before I strap in?

"Why do you let him get away with that shit, boss?" Roach asked, still standing beside him, glaring after Patty as he paced over to the rolling steps and began dragging them back to his mech to boost himself up into the cockpit. She cracked the knuckles of her right hand and made a fist. "You say the word,

I'll take him outside and give him a little kinetic counseling. Maybe then he'll control that damn mouth of his."

"We don't have the luxury of riding his ass too hard, Roach," Nate said, shrugging. "It's not as if I have volunteers lining up around the block to take his job. Until we can get back to one of the enclaves, maybe pick up a couple more pilots, this is all we got and it has to get the job done."

"My Uncle Steve was a Gunny in the USMC, back when it was still around, and he wouldn't have put up with a shithead like him in the Corps," Roach said with a dissatisfied grunt. She pulled on the sleeves of her flight suit and zipped it up. "He'd have had Patty mopping the damn warehouse floor until his hands bled."

Nate glanced down at the dirt and muck visible through the cracked cement of the floor and barked a laugh.

"What about your dad?" he asked her, remembering her father had been in Army Special Forces. "What would he have done?"

The corner of Roach Mata's mouth curled upward, a humorless snarl.

"Dad wouldn't have bothered. He knew when to cut deadweight."

She moved over to her machine, shoulders square and back straight and he felt an involuntary shudder. Roach was a military brat from way back, and sometimes her happy-to-be-here eagerness made him forget just how damned scary she could be.

At least she's on our side.

He stared up at the looming metal and carbon fiber and honeycomb boron of the Hellfire mech and wondered what "our side" meant at this point. Did he even believe that shit about restoring the United States that Dix was pushing? Or was he in it for the money like Patty? There were days he thought he knew, but Norfolk brought out the cynic in him. Just what had the United States ever done for him, other than chew him up and spit him out, over and over, one life after another?

Oh well, whether he did it for the good old US of A, or for their money, or just for the men and one woman of Broken Arrow Mercenary Force, the job had to be done. He pulled the canopy open and grabbed the handholds, pulling himself up. It was a matter of pride not using the steps, even though the strain did nasty things to his shoulder joints.

Getting too old for this shit, he thought, settling into the control chair and strapping in.

I'll be seven next month.

CHAPTER TWO_

It had once been the oldest shipyard in Virginia, maybe in the whole United States. He couldn't remember, if he'd ever known. If the original Nate Stout had ever known. It had sat bestriding the Elizabeth River, a monument to industry and America's commitment to world leadership. Now, the few ships left were rusted hulks, capsized or resting on the river bottom, and little was left of the buildings except chunks of concrete and strips of aluminum sheeting waving in the breeze. Like so much of the old port, it had been razed by the nuclear weapon terrorists had smuggled onto a cargo ship and detonated just off the coast. Here and there, a towering crane still rose in defiance of physics and global politics, and the Jordan River bridge still spanned the green and brown and occasionally blue flow, looking as new as when thousands of cars crossed it every day, but all else was devastation.

And it looks worse from the air.

"We're going down, Dix," he transmitted. "Leave the U-mechs in a patrol pattern."

Nate throttled back his jets and the Hellfire descended from one hundred meters to touch down near the defiant remains of a gantry crane, long faded from its original jaunty, royal blue to something more depressing. Ancient concrete cracked beneath the weight of the machine's footpads and Nate felt the sudden, irrational fear that the whole place would collapse from underneath him. He shifted the Hellfire's weight, running a 360-degree scan of the area as Dix brought his mech down a dozen meters away, closer to the river bank.

"Place looks completely deserted," the former Naval officer said, tracking back and forth across the ruins with the upper torso of his machine.

"It does," Nate admitted reluctantly. "I thought it would make a good transfer point for cargo, though. The tracks in and out are still basically intact." He used his Vulcan to point out at the railroad tracks running from the base of the crane. "And the roads are fairly clear."

"That's the thing about this damned place," Dix said, snorting a humorless laugh, "there are more ports here than anywhere on the Eastern Seaboard. I was stationed here back when, you know?"

"You mentioned it once or twice," Nate replied dryly. *Only every few minutes since we arrived.* "I've been here before myself. Sort of."

"That's gotta be weird, isn't it?" Dix wondered. "Carrying around the memories from your...what do you call it, the original Nathan Stout?"

"The prime," Nate told him, his mouth suddenly going dry. "They called him the prime."

Cold talons gripped his spine and he wanted to hit the thrusters and take off again, run away from Dix and the conversation. Dix was the only one who knew, the only one he'd trusted, and then only because the man had run into a previous version of Nate. He wasn't sure if the others would care, but there was too much riding on keeping BAMF together for him to take the chance.

He shook off the panic, stuffed the fear away into a locked room inside his head the way he always did, and cleared his throat.

"No, it's not weird. Not any weirder than your memories are to you. They just feel like me. The frustrating part is when you know there are things you *should* remember, but you don't, because some asshole in a DARPA research lab decided you didn't *need* your childhood to pilot a Hellfire. That you don't *need* to remember who your wife was..." He trailed off, wincing. "Who your *prime's* wife was," he corrected himself, "when you're only going to live twelve or fifteen years. That's what's weird."

"Shit," Dix murmured. "Sorry, man. Didn't mean to..."

"It's okay. Look, there's something over there." He pointed with the mech's articulated left hand. "I'm not sure if it's part of this shipyard or not, but I see piers and maybe a drydock. Let's check it out."

Thrusters pushed him back into his seat, the pressure and discomfort in his knees and shoulders a welcome distraction. The physical pain reminded him of his mortality, which was easier to deal with than the spiritual pain, the sort that reminded him of his origins, of the fact he was a cheap, disposable copy. Breaking down. Falling apart. Like Norfolk.

Closer to the Jordan River Bridge now, soaring just above it with the U-mechs mirroring their flight a few hundred meters behind. This close, the bridge didn't seem so sturdy, so unchanged. The pilings were intact, but the road surface had eroded away, huge sections cracked and crumbled and just missing, fallen into the river years ago and carried away.

How long? he wondered. How long before the bridge was

washed away on the tides of time, like everything else he'd been fighting to preserve? *Jesus, stop being so damned maudlin.*

He caught sight of a sign above where the traffic lanes used to be, announcing the toll for the bridge was $12. He laughed bitterly, remembering paying that shit every single day. Then the laugh died and the bitterness remained. It wasn't *him* who'd paid the toll, wasn't *him* who'd served in Norfolk.

He concentrated on checking the other side of the river for threats or signs of activity, running his eyes and the thermal scanners over a ragged line of old cargo containers, dropped off a decade ago and never opened. They lined the shore by the hundreds, rusting away.

"Nothing on the scanners still," Dix reported. "You?"

"Negative." He didn't shake his head...that was something you learned, controlling your motions in the cockpit, because the targeting reticle on the missile was slaved to his eyes and the launcher followed the movements of his head. "There's..." He trailed off, spotting something, then touching a control to force the cockpit optics to zoom in on it. "Over there. I'll hit it with a laser designator."

He blinked and the targeting system projected the laser to follow his eyes down to a cluster of seven containers just behind the pier, right at the edge of the railroad tracks.

"See those? The damned paint's not even flaking on them. Someone dropped them off very recently."

"Probably used the rail lines," Dix agreed. "Let's take a closer look."

"No, you stay up here," Nate decided. "I don't want us getting caught with our pants down. I'll take a U-mech down with me."

"You're the boss," he said, though Nate could tell it wasn't an acknowledgement as much as it was a gentle reproof. He was the boss and he shouldn't be taking risks while his subordinates sat back and watched, in other words.

Tough shit. I was literally built to be expendable. Well, grown, not built, but still...

"Everything is clear over here, Boss," Roach said, her voice tinny and distant in his ear. "You want me and Ramirez to head over that way and assist?"

"Negative," he told her, grunting at the jolt up through his the small of his back as the Hellfire touched down again. Behind him, the U-mech landed like a shadow, the cloud of dust from its thrusters merging with the billows from his own. "Maintain position and keep scanning that end of the shipyards. Keep this channel open, though," he added, "and if you hear the sound of shit hitting the fan, you get your asses over here."

She was affirming his orders, but the words were a mosquito-buzz in his ear, shut out by his total focus on what the visual scans of the cargo containers and the railway behind them was showing him. The tracks showed signs of recent braking, the oxidation scraped away in streaks. Someone had used it recently, and...

"Dix, you seeing what I'm seeing?" He used the optical guidance system in his helmet to read where his eyes were focused and sent a laser designator out for his second-in-command.

"Is that...," Dix trailed off and Nate could imagine him squinting at the magnified optics. "Cigarette butts?"

"Bet your ass it is."

They were scattered on the gravel and sand beside the railroad tracks, beside one of the cargo containers near the center. Its right-hand door hung open about a dozen centimeters, tantalizing, and Nate took a step closer, the whine of the hip servos deafening in the sudden silence. Darkness concealed the interior from him and he sidestepped, lining up the spotlight on his shoulder and flicking the switch to activate it.

The angled slice of view he was allowed through the small opening revealed nothing, just bare metal and he muttered a curse.

"I'm going to pull open the left-side door," he warned his cover man. "Don't let the monsters get me, Daddy."

"Roger that," Dix drawled. "And I'll read you a bedtime story and leave the hall light on."

The Hellfire's articulated left hand was more useful than Nate had imagined it would be the first time Bob had showed him the design. He'd argued with the man, wondering why he'd waste the space on the human hand analog when he could have just put in a second rotary cannon, but situations like this showed why Franklin was a filthy-rich weapons designer and Nate Stout was a divorced Army test pilot...

Damn. He'd done it again, got lost in the Prime's memories. *He* had never met Robert Franklin, much less been close enough friends to call him "Bob." Franklin had been dead years before he was "born."

Get your head in the fucking game, Nathan.

He wished he could hold the Vulcan in front of him, but there wasn't room and it would have been overkill for a few dismounts inside a cargo container, so he switched to the 6.5mm machine guns mounted in the mech's chest, kept his finger held straight beside the trigger on the steering yolk and used the waldo controls to rip the left-hand door aside. It opened with the metallic shriek of a lost soul, whipping around to slam against the side of the container, a hollow, booming thud. Under the glare of the spotlight, he could see...

"Nothing," he said. "Empty."

"This could be a dry hole, Nate," Dix warned. "Those butts could have been from days ago. There ain't been no rain and these containers could have been dropped off weeks ago for all we know..."

"You weren't a Captain, were you, Dix?" Nate interrupted him. "In the Navy, I mean?"

"You know I was a Lieutenant, Nate."

"Then stop trying to be Captain Obvious and watch my damn six," he snapped. "I'm opening the next one."

Footpads scraped across the gravel in an awkward sidestep and behind him, the U-mech mirrored his motions in what could have been the world's most expensive and ridiculous dance routine. The damn things would be so much more useful if they had an autonomous AI system, but no one had managed to work the bugs out before everything had gone to shit.

Not that they'd worked the bugs out of genetic duplication either, but that hadn't stopped them from making him and the other dupes. Dupe was a damned good word for it, too. They'd been duped, all right.

The clawed fingers of the Hellfire's hand closed around the latch of the right-hand door on the next cargo container over and Nate shifted the mech's stance, ready to rip the lock apart.

The railcar exploded. In retrospect, Nate would realize only the one end of the container had been rigged with breaching charges, but at the time it sure as hell felt as if the whole damned thing had exploded. The concussion knocked his Hellfire backwards, off-balance, stumbling in stunned concert with its pilot. For once, the U-mech didn't mimic his moves, safety interlocks assuring it would stand its ground when its master unit was attacked.

Nate was yelling incoherently, his stomach doing backflips as he felt the mech collapsing, and only the railcar directly behind it kept him from landing flat on his back and being stuck there like an upturned tortoise, baking in the sun. The U-mech stood watching like that one worthless friend who'd take videos of you falling and post it online before helping you up.

Which put it directly in the line of fire when the Russian Tagan burst out of the remains of the railcar and opened fire with every weapon it had. The machine had a gaunt, stretched-out frame that had always reminded Nate of some sort of creepy, mechanized zombie, more ridiculous than intimidating; but the blinding glare of cannons and missiles launchers discharging in a ceaseless fusillade of yellow and red fire were suddenly damned intimidating. One second, Nate's U-mech was standing there, waiting for input Nate was too stunned to give it, and the next, it was the center of an expanding fireball and pieces of it were pinwheeling into the river on trails of black smoke.

Nate couldn't see a damned thing, not even on thermal; everything was burning metal and thick, dark, roiling clouds of smoke and his targeting systems couldn't get a fix through it. Desperate, he fired a Mark-Ex anti-armor missile blindly and stomped on the thruster controls, blasting backwards into the container behind him. He'd been trying to bounce off the metal railcar, trying to get airborne, but the angle was wrong and instead, he tipped the thing over backwards and himself with it.

The Marx-Ex hit *something*, though God knew what. He felt the detonation in his sinuses, heard the ricochets off his chest plastron just before he flipped backwards, his helmet smacking hard enough against the interior cockpit wall to send stars floating across his vision. Then he was on his left side, or the Hellfire was on its left side, or both; and the roaring was still filling his ears and flashes of light blanked out his view and a hailstorm of dirt and gravel and burning, ragged bits of metal were falling all around him.

Did I get it? I must have gotten it...

Then he heard a long burst of static on his helmet

earphones, nearly drowned out by the chorus of alarms and warnings and alerts sounding in the cockpit. It took him a half-second to focus on the sound, another fraction of a second to pick it out from the feedback as a man's voice, yelling in shock and surprise and maybe pain.

It was Brian Richardson, and he was screaming.

CHAPTER THREE_

"Taking fire!" Richards was screaming. "I've got damage to my port turbine!"

"Hold on!" Nate told him, jamming his left arm forward against the control gimbal, wedging his Hellfire's hand into the gravel and trying to push the mech over onto its stomach, trying to get its legs underneath him. "Roach! Ramirez! Patty! Get your asses over here!"

"On our way, boss!" Roach Mata called. "But we're two mikes out now."

"Well, shit," he murmured, kicking the mech's feet out and trying to roll it back to its feet. "That might be just a bit longer than we have to live."

The haptic resistance of the controls made it almost feel as if Nate were physically lifting the multi-ton Pi-Mech to its feet, and he nearly screamed himself at the white-hot knife of pain in his left AC joint, the chronic bursitis in his shoulder just one of the effects of the gradual degeneration dupes went through as they passed mid-life. But then he was upright, squatting behind the overturned railcar, and he could finally see what was going on.

Brian Richardson's U-mech was crashing into the river in what seemed like slow motion, bits of it tumbling away from the slowly spinning, fiery mass of the torso, fountains of steam hissing off the surface of the water as the burning wreckage hit piecemeal. It had taken a missile; nothing else would have knocked it down so quickly, and Dix was heading down as well. His Hellfire trailed smoke from its portside turbine and the starboard was feathering, either from damage or on purpose, to get him on the ground before he crashed.

But where's the damned Tagan?
Something that big, how the hell could he lose it?
In the smoke, naturally.
Clouds of it were flowing across the dock, over the pier, a smudge across the river, pulled over his vision like an impenetrable veil. The thermal sensors picked up fountains of glaring white everywhere he looked, the lidar useless in the haze of particulates, the radar…
Shit.
The radar showed something big and medal and only ten meters to his right. He planted his mech's left foot and spun toward the threat, trying to bring anything he had to bear on it, but just a fraction of a second too slow. 25mm armor-piercing rounds speared through the smoke, chased by the low chop-chop-chop stutter of the Tagan's chain gun. They weren't as big or as fast or as immediately lethal as the 20mm cannon rounds of his Vulcan, but they were on target and he wasn't.

Armor cracked and splintered along his mech's left shoulder and the concussive vibration shook him like a bone in a dog's mouth. Fighting to keep focus, he switched his weapons control to his missile launcher, trying to get a lock-on with the radar. Warning lights flashed red and the trigger locked hard against his finger—the missile launcher had been hit and now there were several hundred thousand dollars' worth of useless high-explosive ordnance trapped only meters away from him and someone was shooting at it.

He cursed and fire wildly with his 40mm cannons, not expecting to hit anything, but wanting to at least take his shot before the Russian bastard took him out. Amazingly, one of the rounds slammed home somewhere on the Tagan's right torso and it recoiled to the side at the detonation of the explosive round, giving Nate time to move. He lunged against the waldos, throwing his Hellfire to the right, the footpads throwing up sprays of gravel as the long-legged strides ate up ground. Behind him, 25mm shells tore up the ground, each its own miniature mushroom cloud.

"Patty!" he yelled into his audio pickup. "Roach! Ramirez! Goddammit, is *anyone* in range yet?"

He *wanted* to take off, try to fly, get some distance between him and the Tagan, but he couldn't do that. Dix was back there, his mech damaged, and he couldn't abandon him. He had to keep the thing engaged, which meant he had to stay on the ground. He ducked behind another of the cargo containers, weaving in and out of the rusted and time-worn metal railcars as 25mm rounds chopped a trail of sparks and dust and smoke behind him.

Servo motors whined in protest at the strain, joints grinding at each hard turn, data and images scrolling across his sensor screens and his HUD faster than he could follow. He abandoned hope of trying to follow the lidar and radar and thermal readings and just concentrated on his Mk-I eyeballs

What they showed him, just past the line of railcars, just over the rise of the railroad track, was a drydock. Basically a huge pit dug into the ground and lined with concrete, the front end abutted the river and could be flooded to let ships float in, then drained to allow work on the lower hull. It was dozens of meters down and even a mech wouldn't survive a fall to the bottom of it. Maybe if he could draw the Tagan after him, get it on the other side of the drydock, Dix would have time to get out.

He was still debating the idea one second later when a missile from the Russian mech speared through the end of the cargo container he'd just ducked behind, the force of the blast from the warhead ripping half the railcar into metal shrapnel and sending the rest spinning into the air, trailing a halo of black smoke. The concussion slammed into the Hellfire and sent it and him flying and ending the debate. He jammed his thruster control pedals to the floor, trying to keep his mech upright, and shot over the top of the cargo container, taking off at a sharp angle just a few meters off the ground.

The railroad tracks flashed by just beneath his canopy and he came within a meter of colliding with an old power pole. The Tagan didn't miss it, didn't seem to care it was there. The pole shattered in creosote-coated wood splinters at the impact with the Russian mech's shoulder and then Nate was facing forward, lining his mech's body up with the thrusters, aiming for the far side of the drydock.

A missile flashed by him, narrowly missing as he dodged, began to curve back toward him. This time, though, his Hellfire's automated anti-missile systems had time to detect it and the 6.5mm machine guns in his chest swiveled to open fire on the warhead as it corrected its course. The missile went out of control, its guidance system damaged, heading off straight into the sky and self-destructing over a kilometer away.

It can't have many more of the damn things, can it? Nate thought, more a hope than an estimate.

At least it didn't fire another missile before he reached the far side of the drydock and had to touch down before the jets overheated. The Hellfire stomped onto hard concrete, running almost out of control the first few steps before Nate was able to dig the footpads in and turn to meet the oncoming Tagan. He finally had a clear shot and opened fire with his 20mm Vulcan, but the Tagan was head-on, presenting very little cross-section, and twisting and rolling as it flew and he had to hope no innocents were in the path of the heavy slugs for the next few kilometers or they were screwed.

The Vulcan ran dry with a flash of yellow and an awful silence and the Tagan touched down only ten meters in front of him. He had the terrible realization he had seconds to live, and suddenly the six or seven years more of life he'd lamented as too short seemed like an unrealized eternity.

"Hey Boss!" Roach yelled in his ear. "Heads up!"

The Marx-Ex didn't quite hit the Tagan square; the Russian mech had seen it coming and tried to take off to avoid it, but it detonated a meter behind the enemy machine, close enough to Nate to send his Hellfire stumbling backwards under the bombardment of a hail of shrapnel. The Tagan landed hard on its feet, its knees bending nearly to the snapping point, black smoke pouring from its thrusters.

They're skragged, Nate realized, hope and inspiration surging neck to neck in his chest. *He can't fly. But he can fucking well fall.*

The 40mm cannons fired in tandem at his left shoulder, pounding round after round into the Tagan, none of the HE rounds quite enough to pierce its heavy armor, but certainly enough to distract it as he ran forward. He slammed his Hellfire's clawed left fist into the center of the Tagan's chest and grabbed hold, pushing forward with everything his reactor had to give. The Tagan slid backwards, arms flailing, weapons firing at nothing, too close to him to aim.

He couldn't see the edge of the pit below his feet when he gave the final push.

The Tagan looked eerily like a human as it catapulted off the side of the drydock, arms and legs twisting, body rolling, trying to do something, anything to arrest its fall. Nothing would. Years of built up sand and dirt did little to cushion the impact, but it did make an impressive dust cloud when the mech struck the concrete bottom of the pit. The metallic crash echoed back and forth between the walls and then died away. Smoke drifted up from the motionless machine like a soul leaving a body.

And if there's a body in there, it's just as dead.

Nate settled back into his seat, finally able to take a full breath again after what had seemed like hours, and the Hellfire seemed to relax around him, straightening and stepping back from the edge. Beside him, Roach Mata's mech touched down on twin jets from her thrusters, throwing up a spray of dust billowing around them.

"You okay, Boss?" she asked him. She was close enough he could see her worried frown through the mech's canopy.

"Yeah, I'm just fucking peachy," he rasped, mouth suddenly feeling dry. He leaned over to the spout end of a water bladder and took a long swallow. "How's Dix?"

"Ramirez is checking on him now, but he seemed okay. His mech's going to need some work."

"Then let's you and I take a look at that thing," he suggested pointing a mechanical finger down at what was left of the Tagan, "and see who might be inside it."

"Gotcha," she said, her Hellfire lifting slowly off the ground, thrusters roaring.

Nate took a moment longer to steady himself. Violence was his profession, but he couldn't remember the last time he'd been so close to death, even in the memories borrowed from his Prime. He sucked down a deep, shuddering breath and descended into the pit beside his teammate. The Tagan didn't move at their approach, not so much as a last, galvanic twitch of its servos, but Roach still kept her Vulcan aimed at the thing's cockpit.

"You want the honors, Boss?" she asked him, gesturing toward the canopy. It was opaque, unlike the version on their Hellfires, cracked but still basically intact. Nate thought of the deformed, bloody mush of a crushed human body and wanted to order her to open it, but he was out of ammo and she wasn't.

"Right," he grunted. "Don't shoot me."

"Of course not," Roach replied, sounding as if she was scandalized by the notion. "I need this job."

Nate shook his head, wondering what it was like to be that young, then leaned over the Tagan, working the Hellfire's claw hand into the edge of the cockpit canopy. Smoke still hissed upward from the wreckage of the machine's turbines, but it hadn't caught fire. Yet. He strained his core muscles instinctively, even though the Hellfire's servos were doing all the work. The canopy peeled away from the front of the Tagan like the skin off a banana, bits of high-impact plastic flaking away as he yanked the cockpit hatch off its moorings with one final, powerful pull, then tossed it aside.

The cockpit was empty.

Well, no, that wasn't exactly accurate. The cockpit was unoccupied by a human pilot, but it was jammed with remote control communications gear and what looked to him like a fairly sophisticated computer system.

"It was a U-mech?" Roach blurted. "How the hell…I mean…" She stood straight and rotated her mech's torso back and forth, scanning their surroundings. "Where's the master unit? Wouldn't we have noticed another mech flying around here?"

"They didn't use a mech," Nate guessed. He wanted to spit in disgust, but the helmet and the close walls of the cockpit made it problematic. "They probably had a truck with commo gear and a remote-control setup on one of the nearby access roads, or maybe even in a boat."

"Well, fuck," the young woman muttered. "Now what?"

"Contact our support teams and get a barge out here to haul it back to base," he told her. Then he paused, paranoia gnawing at the frayed edge of his nerves. "But yank the GPS tracker first."

He was close enough to see her squinting at him curiously through her canopy.

"Okay, but why bother?"

He did his best not to snap the response back at her, trying to remind himself of her youth and inexperience.

Youth, hell. She was in High School the day I woke up with a migraine that first time.

"Because I don't want whoever planted this thing tracing it back to our base," he explained, grabbing at patience with both hands. "It's bad enough they tracked us here." He let loose of the waldos long enough to run a hand over his face, wiping away the collected sweat. "No one should have known we were here."

Something struck him, like the feeling you've forgotten something but can't remember what it is. Then it hit him and he began searching the sky above the pit.

"And where the hell is Patty, anyway?"

CHAPTER FOUR_

YORKTOWN BEACH HADN'T BEEN that popular even before the war, but back home in Kentucky, Geoff Patterson had never thought he'd ever have a beach to himself. Even a river beach, littered with garbage. The George P Coleman Memorial Bridge stretched highway 17 out over the York River, then gave up on the whole thing halfway across and sank into the wreckage the military had left behind as a deterrent for invaders during the war.

Well, technically, the war ain't over. Except it is and we're just too damned stupid to realize it.

He dropped to the sand, his combat boots sinking into it a couple centimeters. *No, a couple inches. Fuck you, metric system. I'm from Kentucky, I ain't using that shit.*

He pulled off his helmet and let it drop to the sand with casual negligence. It was cooler here than it had been in Norfolk, trapped inside that damned warehouse at the docks, sweating his ass off every day, banging their heads against a wall chasing phantom Russian saboteurs.

"Do I gotta go back?" he wondered aloud.

"For now," came the answer from over his left shoulder. He looked back, unsurprised. She was why he'd come.

Her voice was low and sultry and she had a face to match, high cheekbones and high forehead, her blond hair pulled back tightly against her scalp only to cut loose in a wild mane across her shoulders. Her tan sweater and matching skirt hugged her slender figure as if she'd been poured into them, and she seemed as if she gave no thought to the dirt and sand coating her designer boots.

"This is an interesting place," she said, her hand brushing against his shoulder as she passed him, a touch of fire even through his Nomex flight suit. "So much of your history began here."

"Is that why you wanted to meet here?" He stepped up just behind her, close enough to feel the warmth, for strands of hair blown on the breeze to tease at his face. "I thought it was 'cause there was no surveillance drone coverage in this area."

"That too," she admitted. She waved a hand around them and he admired the perfect manicure, the spotless skin. She wasn't exactly young, had to be somewhere in her thirties at least, but damned if he could spot any sign of her age even from this close. "This is where the British forces surrendered to the Colonials during your War for Independence, you know?"

He shrugged.

"I s'pose. I ain't much of a history buff. Back home, I had more important things to learn just to stay alive." Like how to hijack a truck and get the load squirreled away and then torch the rig before the police drones spotted you.

"Your people call it the Revolutionary War," she said, and she leaned back into him. The feel of her body against his was an electric surge straight to his heart and then lower. "It is a misnomer. A revolution is the overthrow of an existing government in favor of a new one. Yours was a colonial war for independence from the mother country. Do you know why this matters, Geoffrey?"

"I can't say as I do, Svetlana," he admitted. "But if you say it's important, then it is."

She laughed, rich and throaty and enough to make his belly turn backflips.

"It is because revolutions come at times when things are bad and make them worse. Violent revolutions *never* lead to more freedom, to better conditions, to better rulers. They only lead to death and destruction and tyranny. In Russia, we revolted against the Czars in 1917 because we were desperate, because things seemed as if they could not get any worse. And yet they did. Once the Bolsheviks gained power, they began to kill off those they deemed not pure enough in their beliefs, and in the end, hundreds of millions died and things were so much worse and lasted so much longer than it should have. And we were not able to free ourselves of the Communists for decades."

She turned, her hands going to his chest, her breath warm against his cheek. "The same was true of the French Revolution. They overthrew their king and thought they would be instituting a new sort of republic that gave power to the average person, but in reality, it was the start of a purge where those not considered pure enough were killed by the tens of thousands, and a new military dictator rose up, Napoleon, to plunge the world into war."

"That's all nice and depressing," he said, hands at the small of her back, daring, pressing her against him. "But that ain't why I'm here."

"You are here because of this," she said, and she kissed him.

She tasted like cherries and cigarette smoke and he started thinking about the buildings still standing on the beach, wondering if any of them was clean enough inside to suit.

"Easy, my Geoffrey," she cautioned pushing a hand against

his chest when he began to grind against her. "We are not beasts to rut in the dirt. We will meet again for that, when the time and place are right."

He tried to get his breathing under control, tried to cap the rising flood inside his chest, but it wasn't easy. And once he'd stopped thinking with his little head, the big one had far too much on its mind.

"What's gonna happen to them?" he wanted to know.

"You need not concern yourself," she said, something cold in her voice rather than the reassurance he'd sought. She seemed to notice the effect her words had and she sighed, almost in disappointment. "The orders were to try to avoid killing them. Accidents may happen, but harming them is not our intent."

"I didn't want it to come to this," he insisted, tilting his head back into the sun and closing his eyes. "They can be assholes sometimes, but they're still my friends. I just...my family..."

"They are deceiving themselves. They believe they can save something that has already been lost. The world that was will never come back, just as the days of the Czars and the Communists and the world of the British Empire are all lost to the tides of history."

She nodded toward the broken bridge, the abandoned buildings crumbling in the sun.

"All this will be swept away and replaced by something new, and this new thing will not be the America they wish to save. The time of countries is past. Now the world is controlled by those who know how to exploit its resources at maximum efficiency."

"So, you don't work for the Russians, then?" It was a verbal jab. She was incredibly hot, but she could get so damned full of herself sometimes. He crossed his arms over his chest and regarded her skeptically. "You don't want to take control of the

Eastern Seaboard so they can have an uncontested port for their ships to unload?"

"I didn't say it was *only* on your side that men misread history," she admitted, chuckling. "What the Federation government believes I do here and what I actually do are two different things. The man who I truly work for does not wish a revolution, Geoffrey. He wishes a war for independence, not merely from *a* country, but from *all* countries."

She took his hand and turned him back to the beach. "The men who fought the British were considered traitors, you know. But they were on the right side of history."

He blew out a heavy sigh and shook his head.

"Then maybe there's hope for me, yet."

Nate wasn't sure where Dix had gotten the cigar, but he sure as hell seemed to be enjoying it. The former Naval officer sat on the chest of his mech as if it were a bull elephant he'd taken down on safari, prone and strapped down to tie-downs on the flat deck of the remotely-sailed barge. Dix leaned back and blew out an aromatic cloud of smoke, then watched the ocean breeze carry it away before he clambered to his feet and hopped off the barge and up onto the dock beside their warehouse just as the rubber fender scraped up against the pilings.

Nate cut thrusters and felt a jolt as his Hellfire lowered the last two centimeters to the surface of the pier. He cracked open his canopy and pushed it upward, letting in the breeze. Dark clouds were swelling shoreward from the ocean, the brisk, fresh air carrying away the stink of the bay but promising the storm to come.

"Ramirez," he called into his throat mic. "Go get the crane

and get the Hellfire and what's left of the Tagan inside the warehouse before they start attracting attention."

"Got it," the young man responded, perhaps just a bit of sullen resentment in his tone. Nate grinned, since the boy couldn't see it. Being the team "mule" was a bitch, but they'd all had to do it when they were the junior man. Well, *he* hadn't done it, but rank had its privileges.

"Hey Dix," he called down to the man, "I thought celebratory cigars were meant for when you *win* a fight, not when you get your ass kicked and your mech trashed."

"Any fight you walk away from is a win," Dix replied with a phlegmatic shrug, then shot him a bird before tossing the cigar stub away and heading into the warehouse.

It felt odd walking in the mech with the canopy open, the difference between operating a convincing simulator and flying an open-cockpit biplane at low altitude. The swaying, rocking gait of the mech felt precarious, like walking on stilts, and he nearly pulled the canopy shut again but forced himself not to. Fears got faced, not avoided. His life was too short to let fear run it.

Without the light amplification of his cockpit optics, he had to pause in the doorway to let his eyes adjust. When they did, he saw the Hellfire nestled in one of the service bays, Geoff Patterson standing at its feet, leaning casually against it. He stiffened, fighting an urge to drop out of the canopy and go slam the tall man up against the wall. Instead, he calmly stepped the mech over to its assigned service bay and backed in, locking the feet into position before he powered the machine down and yanked loose his restraints. He'd hoped to be the first to confront Patterson, but Dix was already there and already on foot and had more reason than any of them to be pissed off.

"Where the *fuck* were you, Patty?" Dix's bellow echoed off the sheet metal walls as he stalked across the warehouse floor, jabbing a finger toward the younger man. "My happy ass was swinging in the breeze and we were yelling for backup and where the fuck *were* you?"

Nate opened the hatch at his feet and slid down quickly, wincing in anticipation at how bad the hard landing was going to hurt his knees. He wasn't disappointed and it took him a moment with his eyes closed and teeth grinding together before he could straighten and limp over to where Dix was confronting Patty.

"I couldn't get there in time," Patty said. He sounded subdued, defensive. He couldn't meet Dix's eyes. "I was only halfway there when I heard it was all over and you were calling in a barge, so I just headed back to base."

"And you didn't think about checking in with us?" Nate asked him, hobbling over to wedge himself between the two men before Dix took a swing at Patty. Dix's face was starting to turn red, his lips pressed together. He was a hard man to get angry, so it was a sort of an accomplishment. "Maybe a radio call to tell us you weren't burning in a ditch somewhere after a Russian ambush?"

"I tried," he insisted, his voice convincingly contrite but his eyes still on the floor. "I think maybe someone was jamming in the area."

"That's a crock of shit and you know it," Roach declared, stalking up from behind them.

Great. Just when I was getting Dix calmed down, now she's spun up, too.

The woman edged past Nate and got into Patty's face...well, as close as into his face as she could get when she was a head shorter.

"You know damn well you were off shamming somewhere, trying to avoid getting into the fight! Just that one damned remotely piloted Tagan took out Dix and two U-mechs. What if they'd had two or three of them? Nate and Dix could be fucking dead now!"

"Back off!" Patty yelled, leaning in closer, finally getting pissed off. "I don't answer to you and I don't have to prove anything to you! I was trying to help and you guys had me too far away from your position! You want me to come hold your fucking hand after a fight so you don't get the shakes, then buy me fucking dinner!"

Nate saw the shift of Mata's feet, the redistribution of weight that was a prelude to throwing a punch, and he stepped between the two of them in a smooth, slithering motion he'd learned from an old NCO. *Well,* someone *had learned it.*

"That'll be enough of this shit." He tried to project firm authority and wasn't sure how successful he was. "We just got our asses kicked out there, ambushed. Someone knew where our AO was, and that means we have a leak."

"Three guesses who ran their mouth," Roach spat the words at Patty. "And the first two don't count."

"I *said,* enough," Nate snapped. "Patty," he ground out, not looking at the man, eyes fixed on Roach lest she try something stupid, "go help Ramirez with the crane, get that shit in here ASAP."

The tall Kentuckian grunted acknowledgement and brushed past the two of them, heading out to the pier at a sulky drag. Dix said nothing, just watched the younger man go and then stuck his hands in his pockets and headed back to the bunk room. Nate wasn't worried about Dix; he was a professional and he'd blow it off after he'd had a chance to cool down. Roach, though...

"You need to get rid of him," she told Nate, jerking a thumb over her shoulder at the door where Patty had exited. "He's ten kilos of shit packed in a five-kilo sack and I will never fucking trust him. How the hell do you even work with the *carbon*?"

"We take what we can get," he reminded her, leaning back against the wall to take some of the pressure off his abused knees. "It's my job to make the team I have work."

"Yeah, but only four of us are working, Boss." She hissed out a breath and closed her eyes, visibly trying to bleed off the rage she'd built up. When she met his gaze again, it was with a calmer visage, but not a kind one. "You're going to have to cut bait sooner or later. Hopefully, it's before his screw-ups gets somebody killed."

He didn't know how to respond to that, so it was almost a relief when the woman turned and headed out the door to the pier. Nate let his head rest against the wall, suddenly feeling very tired. He thought about heading back to his rack and trying to grab a nap, but his Hellfire glared at him accusatorily, still ragged and burned and splintered, waiting to be serviced.

"Serves me right," he murmured, limping over to the machine, "for being too cheap to hire a maintenance team."

INTERLUDE_

I woke up with a splitting headache, like the worst migraine you ever had multiplied by the kind of hangover you got from mixing cheap, Mexican beer and cheaper Russian vodka.

What the hell had I done to myself last night? I couldn't even remember. I slapped at my phone, trying to turn off the blaring alarm without opening my eyes and heard a clatter as it went off the nightstand to clatter on the floor.

"Shit."

I swung my legs out of the bed, flinching a little at the feel of the cold tile on my feet as I leaned down and picked up the phone, opening my eyes just enough to squint at the screen. It wasn't the alarm, it was a call. I'd muted the ringer when I went to bed, but this was the sort of call that wouldn't let you mute it.

I slid the green button to the right to answer and put the phone against my right ear. The pain was beginning to fade now, thank God, or I wouldn't have even been able to hear the voice on the other end.

"Stout here," I said, my mouth feeling as if a sheep had crawled inside it and died last night.

"Stout, report to the hangar ASAP."

"Why, what's..." I trailed off, realizing whoever it was had hung up.

I didn't recognize the voice, but that didn't mean anything. Clerks, technicians, staffers all rotated in and out of here constantly.

Here. Where is here, again? Jesus, I must have really tied one on last night.

I knew where the hangar was, though, and I knew where the light switch was. I tapped the side of the lamp, wincing at the glare of the LED, but following its glow to my flight suit, hanging where it always did on the door of my closet. I slipped into it quickly, fingers working zippers and Velcro fasteners on their own, without conscious thought. My boots were arranged in the usual spot, hanging open so I could just step into them and tighten the straps.

My mouth was still dry and disgusting so I risked the extra thirty seconds to brush my teeth at the sink beside the door, then the water running reminded me I had to pee, so I did that, too and hoped the extra delay wasn't the difference between saving the day and the end of the world. If it was, fuck 'em. A man's gotta do what a man's gotta do.

I didn't hear any alarm klaxons when I opened the door of my quarters, so we weren't under attack, which was always a plus. Maybe it was a drill. I checked the time on my phone: 0415. Just about the time the fuckers would call a drill, when everyone had to get up in an hour.

People were running through the hallways, still fastening fatigue blouses or pulling on tactical vests, some of them with carbines slung over their backs and wearing helmets. The lights were still dimmed, giving the thin sheet rock walls a more solid and substantial look, a sense of permanence they lacked when you saw them in the stark light of day.

Every military base looked the same and I felt as if I'd been stationed at every one of them. This one could have been in California or Texas or South Carolina or just about anywhere except Hawaii or Florida because it was too chilly for that. I glanced out of the side of my eye at a short, stocky woman jogging about the same speed and direction I was. She wore Army utilities and a helmet that looked too big for her head, and she clutched at her M37 rifle as if it were the only life preserver in a stormy sea. Dark eyes flickered my way but she quickly looked away, as if she didn't want to engage.

Had I already developed a reputation here? Had it been that long? Maybe I'd gotten drunk last night and hit on her and she was embarrassed to talk to me. I'd have to ask Bob when I saw him. Hadn't I gone out with Bob last night? Or maybe it had been the night before.

I was at the hangar, so I put last night out of my head, wishing I could get rid of the headache as easily. The lights in the hangar were bright, but they were also higher up, giving them the illusion of a softness they didn't possess. The far-away lamps threw long shadows from the line of Hellfires cradled in their berths, surrounded by maintenance gantries, power cables and diagnostic equipment. The other pilots were already here and I felt like a shit-heel for being so late. They were absorbed in prepping their machines, not even sparing me a glance as I jogged up.

I hesitated a few steps away from my Hellfire, staring at one of them. A woman, quite attractive, with bobbed red hair and a sort of pixie cuteness to her face. And yet, she looked inexplicably...old. Weathered. It didn't seem to fit with her hands, her hair, her build and it was nothing as overt as face cracked by the wrinkles of old age. It was more of a beat-up, worn sense I got from her motions, the way you'd expect someone to move when they got to that age where everything hurt. Her uniform advertised her as a captain, just like me. She shouldn't have been older than thirty, tops; but if you'd asked me, I'd have been willing to swear she was on the downside of the hill.

Strange.

"Stout!"

That was Charlie, loud and bellicose as always, hands perpetually stained with grease and grit, a streak of it across his right cheek. A lump of chewing tobacco bulged at his lower lip, drawing his mouth in what looked like a perpetual snarl.

"I'm here, Charlie," I assured him, clambering up the stepladder and pulling the hatch open. "Is she ready?"

"What do I look like, your fucking turn-down service?" He laughed harshly, then picked up a plastic cup from his toolbox and spat into it. "Of course she's ready! Get your ass inside before you make me look bad."

"Any word on the mission?" I called down to him as I squeezed through the hatch and grabbed a handhold.

"Nothin'," he grunted. "I was called here just like you, I just showed up earlier."

I snorted as I strapped in, grabbing my helmet off the armrest of the seat.

"I stopped to brush my fucking teeth, Charlie. Maybe you should try it sometime."

"The brass'll tell you what's up when you're sealed in." Charlie banged on the outside fuselage and began closing the hatch. "Good luck."

"I don't need luck," I assured him, flicking the power feed switches upward, the turbines beginning to spin to life with a slowly building whine.

"All Hellfire units, this is Combat Control." I heard the voice in my headphones almost the instant I set my helmet on and fastened the chinstrap. The tone was familiar even if the voice wasn't. "We have incoming enemy traffic at seven kilometers due south. Two full squadrons of Russian Tagans on their way. We have intelligence they were launched from a ship off Savannah."

Okay, I was in Georgia. Ft. Stewart, or what was left of it. I remembered now. How could I have forgotten? What the hell was wrong with my head?

"Stout, you take First Squadron and circle to the south, catch them over open ground before they have a chance to target us."

"Got it," I confirmed, not really listening as they gave orders to my counterpart in Second. She was supposed to head north, and I didn't need to know anything more unless she needed support, and then I'd hear plenty.

"First Squadron, hit your jets," I told them. I could see their names on the IFF display, Reynolds, Washburn and Rivers, but for some reason, I couldn't picture their faces. "Let's get them before they get us."

The hangar door was rumbling open, screeching intermittently as if in pain when the rollers hit a rough spot on the track. The cold grey of predawn hung over the old airstrip, transforming the shapes of helicopters tied down on the tarmac into shadowy, fearsome gargoyles of a lost world.

They were still useful for transportation, but in combat trials against mechs, it was no contest. Fighter jets were still the clear champion, of course, but those were just too damned expensive. Mechs were the king of the hill now, for however long that would last.

Probably as long as this war lasts. Which may be until the most advanced weapon around is a rock.

The helicopters watched in envious silence as their replacements cruised out of the hangar on jets of superheated air. I led the squadron up to their cruising altitude of a hundred meters and top speed of a hundred knots, which didn't seem like much until you considered you were flying a tank with arms and legs three hundred feet off the ground at a hundred and twenty miles an hour. Then it seemed really fucking badass.

We curled around what used to be called the Hunter Army Airfield—*How do I know that but can't remember what the other pilots in my squadron look like?*—over endless forests of oaks hung with Spanish moss. I remembered going on field training exercises, brushing aside the moss like bead curtains in the parlor of some old-time fortune teller.

When was that? How many years ago?

We were heading out towards Shellman Bluff, that was what the tactical overlay said. Shellman Bluff, Sapelo Island. I could remember images from them. Bridges over inlets, fishing boats. Little hole-in-the-wall restaurants with excellent food, my wife and I laughing over beers after...

My wife? Where the hell was my wife?

"Stout, you guys okay up there?"

That was Combat Control. Still couldn't remember the woman's name.

"Fine," I told her. "We're about five minutes out from the projected intercept."

"Don't let them through, Stout." There was genuine concern in her voice, which did nothing for my confidence. "This is the third attack just this month. They took out NAS Jax back in October with a nuke they hauled in on a cargo helicopter after they took out the mech wing there just like this."

"Roger that, Combat Control. No pressure."

I kept an eye on the heat readings, not wanting the thrusters to redline before we even got into the fight, deciding somewhere on the outskirts of Shellman Bluff to take us down. We landed in a residential street in some subdivision called something-something Cove. I couldn't make out the top of the sign from the moss hanging over it. The houses looked expensive, or like they had been expensive back in the day, back before civilians had been forced to evacuate the southeastern coastline. Now, they were faded and cracked, roofs covered in moss and tree branches and leaves piled up over the course of years.

Oh, there were still people on the coasts, ones who'd hidden from the military or wandered back in after the patrols were past. They lived in clusters, fishing for a living, trading their catch for fuel for their boats and their generators. About a third of the country was living on a barter economy now, either because of hyperinflation or just lack of infrastructure.

I blinked, not halting my Hellfire in its steady clomp down the cracked and pitted streets but shaking my head and trying to focus. All that information felt as if someone else had dumped it into my brain. How did I know all that but couldn't remember where I was until someone told me? Where the hell was my wife?

Where was Bob? Bob should have been there when we took off. The Hellfires were his babies. Wait. How many Hellfires did we have? Bob's lab had been out west, not in Georgia. How the hell did I even *get* here?

"We ready to fly again, Captain?" Rivers asked me.

I glanced down at the solid green on the heat display and nodded, then realized he couldn't see me.

"Back in the air," I ordered. "We'll stay up till we find them this time."

We were getting close to the water. I could see the saltwater marshes passing by beneath us, the gold of first light beginning to burn away the grey shadows. Flocks of water birds passed by above and below us, cattle egrets, storks, pelicans, going about their business as if the world wasn't spiraling into chaos and destruction. So many people had died, so many were dying every day. Would nature move back in and take over from us when we were gone? Or had we ruined too much of it in our death spasms?

"There they are." Rivers again. The man was talkative. He was also right. I could see the radar blips now, eight Tagans in all.

The Russian mechs were an odd duck. They carried heavier armor than we did, making them slower, but they also had a longer flight time before they had to worry about overheating. Rumor had it they managed that by cutting back on the reactor shielding and their pilots only had a lifespan of about four years once they started regular exposure. After that, the effects would accumulate and cancer or radiation poisoning would make them too sick to fly.

That seemed wasteful to me. How were you going to keep getting motivated volunteers if they rotated out of the pilot's chair after just four years, training included? But these were Russians we were talking about, so I hadn't ruled the story out completely.

Anyway, the long and short of it was, we had the advantage of speed and heavier weapons and they had range and more armor. And they had twice as many in their formation as we did, which was never good.

"Second Squadron," I called, trying to keep the urgency out of my voice. Pilots didn't do urgent or desperate or scared. We *felt* it sometimes, but we never showed it on the radio. "I have located the bogies. Come around to our position and back our play."

"Roger, First," the Second Squadron leader acknowledged, her voice just as phlegmatic as mine had been. "We will be in range in two mikes."

Which was eternity in combat, but never mind, here we were.

"Washburn and Reynolds," I ordered, "split left. Rivers, you're with me on the right. Launch missiles as soon as you're in range, but don't latch until Second gets here. Just keep 'em occupied."

I didn't wait for an acknowledgement, just curled around to the right, about eighty meters above a sheltered inlet. The brown wooden lozenges of boats floated by, sporadically visible through the trees, and I wondered if the people down there knew who was fighting above them or even cared. For them, the United States had been gone for years and all this was just the death throes.

Years? Had it been years? I wanted to say it had been longer...

I got tone and launched, diving below them immediately, hoping Rivers would go by the plan and not get himself shot down before the fight even started. Insistent beeping told me the Russians had fired off a pair of missiles at me, but I was coming up right into the middle of their formation and the birds wouldn't lock with so many friendly IFF signatures in the neighborhood. I wasn't worried about their missiles, but the 25 mike-mike stuttering towards me was another story. Red dashes ignited the morning air, like Morse code signals saying "fuck you, Yankee," and I got the message.

"Stay tight," I warned Rivers. "Don't give them space."

"I'm good," he insisted and I didn't have time to rubberneck and make sure he wasn't lying.

The lead Russian squadron was splitting, trying to catch us in a crossfire, and I had to make a coin-flip call which pair to stay with. I was right-handed, so I spun right, getting directly between the two of them, trying to keep them from being able to fire. Somewhere off to the left, my missile warhead exploded, though I couldn't be sure whether it had gone off of its own volition or been shot down by anti-missile fire.

Tone again and I fired off another bird, closer this time, only a hundred and fifty meters from the Tagan to my front, barely within minimum arming distance for the Xyston missile. This one definitely hit, and when it did, it blew the Russian mech out of the air, sent it tumbling down toward the inlet in a smoking, roiling inferno.

Splash one, but unfortunately, that meant the guy behind me had no reason not to launch his own missiles now. There was no way I was going to be able to get him under my guns in time, and I sure as hell wasn't going to trust my life to Rivers, so I dove. We were only about sixty meters up, I had to cool down my thrusters pretty soon, and damned if there was much land around directly beneath me. I could see the shallows, could tell by radar and lidar pings how deep they were and I knew this thing was watertight.

All I needed was something to put between me and the missiles the threat display assured me were dogging my tail, and I found it in an old, abandoned boathouse at the end of a partially-collapsed dock. Corroded sheet metal covered the dock and served as a roof for the boathouse, discolored and stained with decades of bird shit. It looked like a good, stiff breeze could knock it over, but it had lasted here on the Atlantic coast for this long without falling to hurricane winds and I had to bet it was sturdy enough to set off a missile warhead.

I dropped into the water on the other side of the boathouse, steam hissing up in a roiling cloud above me as red-hot thruster cowlings hit the winter-cool seawater of the inlet. My Hellfire was still sinking chest-deep when the missiles slammed into the other side of the boathouse. It was close—way too close, close enough I could feel the heat through the water and through the cockpit, close enough the sound battered me like a physical blow and the flash blinded me even through the polarized canopy.

The concussion sent my mech drifting sideways and I could hear the metal hailstorm of fragments from the boathouse pinging off the machine's right shoulder just before it sank beneath the surface. Heat levels were dropping down into the green, but I didn't just sit there and watch them; there was still work to do. I dug one foot, then the other into the sand at the bottom of the inlet, pushing the mech up and out of the water in three long steps.

I stomped the throttle pedals and shot up into the air again, an explosion of steam and spraying saltwater marking my launch from the shallows at the edge of the inlet. The boathouse was gone, just a jumble of smoldering wooden pilings, and the dock had collapsed the rest of the way into the water, just one more piece of the past sinking into the waves of time.

I half-expected to see Rivers heading the same way, but I was surprised to find his mech only half a kilometer from mine, running slowly and awkwardly down the strand beside the inlet. When I hit the jets, so did he, pulling up into a trailing echelon beside me.

"Where's the Tagan that launched on me?" I asked him, scanning radar. I hoped I hadn't let him get past me toward the base. It would be a bitch trying to catch up with him.

"He's toast," Rivers told me. "I splashed him right after he launched."

"I take back everything I was thinking about you, Rivers," I told him, grinning. "Come on, let's see what damage we can do."

Reynolds and Washburn were still in one piece, at least according to their transponders, and so were five of the Tagans. Three down already. Not bad.

Our guys were on the ground and so were two of the Russians, sniping at each other from opposite sides of a strand across the pothole-pocked remnant of an old road. The other three Tagans were in a tight formation, three kilometers west of us, heading in a steep descent toward solid ground.

"They're about to hit the forest and try to lose us," I said. "Second Squadron, where the hell are you?"

"Patience, newbie," the woman, Captain Lindquist by her transponder signal, told me. "Check your screens, we're heading right for the bogies."

And they were. I reddened a bit at the "newbie" crack, but now wasn't the time. Second was less than a kilometer north of the Russian formation, and I could see radar blips as they launched a spread of missiles on the way in.

"We got this," Lindquist assured me. "Go help your people."

"Roger that, Second." I switched frequencies. "Follow me in, Rivers."

I couldn't get a target lock for a missile through the trees, and there was a damned good chance the warheads wouldn't keep it anyway with our own guys so close down there. Time for a good old-fashioned knife fight.

"Washburn, Reynolds, we're coming in," I told them. "Don't fucking shoot us."

"No promises," Reynolds said, her voice taut with the stress of the fight but still playful. "I don't know you that well yet."

Yet? Newbie? What were they talking about? Hadn't I been assigned here for months now?

The Tagans had noticed us coming in and one of them tried to launch a missile, but he didn't get a clean lock through the thick tree branches overhead and the Russian junk went soaring past us both, destined for the open water. I ignored it and fed him a long burst of 20mm, which wouldn't discriminate between tree and mech, just speared through one on the way to the other. Wood fragments exploded downward and limbs fell, and so did the Russian.

The last one tried to run, tried to blast away on thrusters, but he was too slow, or maybe Rivers was too fast. My wingman launched a missile the second the Tagan cleared the trees and at this range, there was no avoiding the Xyston. It blew the Russian mech into scrap metal, the burning, smoking bits of what remained splashing into the shallows beside the road.

I touched down in the middle of the old road, Rivers landing only meters away to my right and just behind me. He was a decent wingman for all his griping earlier.

"Everyone okay?" I asked the others. "Any damage?"

"Only to my pride," Washburn said, sounding miffed she hadn't nailed one of the Tagans without our help. "Thanks, Stout. That was a damn good job for a dupe right out of the tanks."

"Your migraine even go away yet?" Rivers wondered.

Ice crept down the veins of my arms and up the arteries to my brain and a veil of unreality fell across my perceptions. Suddenly, I *knew*. I *knew* what I was and I knew *when* was and the bottom seemed to fall right out of the world.

But Charlie...Charlie had known me. He'd treated me like he knew me.

He knew the last one. The one before you. The one that got itself killed.

"First Squadron," Combat Control said and I barely heard the words. "We are detecting an incoming signal, intermittent and coming in low just three kilometers north of your current position. We think it's a stealth helicopter coming in from the coast. It has to be the Russians. Intercept immediately."

"Shit." Helicopter. Hadn't control said something about the Russians smuggling a nuke in with a helicopter in Jacksonville? "Come on!"

I hit thrusters, pushing the redline to get there in time, not even checking the screen to see if they were following me. My eyes were only on the radar blip of the chopper, just the slightest shadow. I would have thought it was a false reading if Combat Control hadn't already put a red enemy icon over it on my threat display. It was moving, but not fast. It was carrying a heavy load. Counting on the Tagans to distract us.

Did it even have a crew or was it remotely piloted? Would the Russians trust something like this to the vagaries of a remote control signal or a pre-programmed autopilot? I'd find out soon, when it detected us coming in on it. I got missile lock, but I'd have to wait until it was in range. Maybe another minute at our relative speeds.

If it was a nuke, would my missile set it off? I wasn't a fucking physicist and I had no idea. Should I ask Control? What the hell would they tell me, don't shoot it, just let it come on in and blow us up?

"Status, First Squadron?" Her voice was nagging and I wanted to snap back until I realized she would be just as scared and uncertain as I was.

"Forty seconds till intercept," I told her. "I have missile lock, waiting for range."

"Roger that. Good luck."

Good luck, she says. If I had good luck, I wouldn't be the latest in a long line of dupes popped out of a tank in a lab.

The other pilots, they'd all be the same as me. We were knock-offs, cheap copies like those fake Gucci purses they used to sell on the streets of New York, and we'd last just as long. It wouldn't matter that the radiation leaking from the mech reactors would kill us in twenty years from cancer because we'd be dead in twelve anyway.

Why did we do it? Why did we keep fighting without being given a choice?

Because they made sure to only duplicate believers, patriots. And they only included memories to reinforce that, not the ones where we were doubting it all. Bastards.

And I knew the other versions of me had thought all this, too, and still did their duty. And so would I.

Bastards.

The targeting reticle flashed green.

"Launching," I announced, squeezing the trigger before I spoke the word.

I could see the helicopter now, sleek and black and curved like a dragonfly. It had a feral beauty to it and I almost hated I was going to destroy it. I guess the Russians hated that too, the damned spoilsports, or else they figured this was close enough to the base.

The exploding heart of a star erupted less than a kilometer away and everything went white.

Better luck next time.

CHAPTER FIVE_

Nate Stout couldn't sleep. He'd been told insomnia was a symptom of genetic degradation, a byproduct of his abbreviated lifespan, but he thought of it as a desperate attempt to cram more experience into fewer years. Usually he thought that. Tonight, he would really just like to have gotten some rest. Stubborn, he tried to keep his eyes closed, but the light leaking in under the window shade was a magnet, drawing his attention even through eyelids squeezed shut. It navigated the tiny bunkroom with the thoroughness of a lidar scan, probing the folds of the shower-curtain dividers they'd hung to divide the space into thirds and the tarps that served as a roof to keep out the moisture and bat shit from the high ceiling of the old warehouse.

He wondered if maybe he'd nodded off and hadn't realized it, but a check of his watch told him it was wishful thinking. It was 0230 and the last time he'd looked, it had been 0158. Two meters away, Dix snored peacefully, as if he hadn't nearly died a few hours ago. No sweating night terrors for that man.

Well, the vodka probably helped.

There'd been a fifth originally, but what remained in the

bottle sitting on Dix's nightstand was about a third of a fifth, which was...

Shit. Can't do that in my head.

Nate sighed, sitting up and swinging his legs over the side of the bed. He reached over and grabbed the bottle, sloshing the clear liquid around the bottom third of it. He unscrewed the cap and took a small swig, grimacing as it burned its way down his throat and settled like smoldering lump of coal into his stomach, heavy and uncomfortable. He could finish it off. He'd sleep then, sure as shit, and regret the hell out of it in the morning.

He'd worked hung over before, in his *own* memory not his Prime's. Sometimes it was harder to deal with the facts of his life than others and alcohol was easier to acquire than other drugs. But the facts would still be there in the morning, when the buzz was long gone and the misery remained.

He'd worked without sleep before, too, and while it was still miserable at least it involved less physical pain. He set the bottle back down and pushed off the cot. It squeaked in protest, only settling down once his weight was off it and back onto his damned knees. He picked through the collection of odds and ends on the nightstand and found a bottle of ibuprofen, popping the cap and pouring out eight of them, then downing them with another swallow of vodka.

That shit would be bad for his liver in the long run, if he had one.

He was dressed in shorts and a t-shirt and he considered just slipping into some flip-flops, but shit always happened when you were least prepared, so he pulled on fatigue pants and combat boots instead and grabbed the gun belt hanging off the end of the cot. It was an old Glock, the slide's finish worn and faded from decades of use, but it still functioned and the ammo was cheap to fabricate. You could get 9mm from any street-corner vendor.

He buckled the Glock around his waist and pushed through the shower curtain into the main floor of the warehouse. The Hellfires brooded in the shadows, ever watchful, their isotope reactors pouring out heat twenty-four-seven, whether they were using it or not. The man-made isotopes were expensive as hell, each fuel cell costing more than the mech it powered, and the radioactivity they generated would kill you just as sure as a missile, which was why the shielding was even more expensive than the fuel cell. It had only been developed in the last ten years, only widespread in the last six or seven.

The deadliness of the radiation was the reason for his existence. Even with the war, the government hadn't been able to justify sticking soldiers in a weapon that would give them terminal cancer with even the best shielding available at the time. Then someone had come up with the brilliant idea to make the dupes, disposable soldiers for a vital weapon in the war against the Russians. It had probably seemed like an acceptable solution in a world where nukes were taking out US cities, delivered not by ICBMs the missile defense system could have brought down but smuggled in by terrorists, mercenaries hired by the Russians.

He probably could have lived with that, could have accepted his fate as a vital cog in the war effort, a last-ditch attempt to save what was left of the United States...but then, around the same time he emerged from the gestation tank, the new shielding had been developed and anyone could fly a mech without worrying about frying their nads off. He was cut loose, given a payout and told to fend for himself.

What the hell does it say about me that I used the money to start BAMF?

He felt the mechs staring at him when he turned his back on them and paced through the grease and dust to the back door. It required an access code to open from either side because he wasn't the most trusting soul even when the gear was subsidized by the Department of Defense, and all the entrances were monitored by infrared and thermal cameras hooked up to a sophisticated security system keyed with each of their biometric data. If anyone not in the databanks tried to enter, with or without the access code, it would set off an alarm.

It wasn't enough. They *really* needed round-the-clock guards, but that would have meant hiring more people and then *trusting* those people, which was an even harder commodity to part with than the money. So they made do with what they had. He punched in his code and pulled the door open.

The storm had passed in a paroxysm of violent, wind-blown rain and thunder hours ago, leaving the pier with a rare, washed-clean smell. It would all go to hell again when the sun came up, would go back to smelling like days-old shit and rotten eggs, but for now he could almost bear it. The clouds had blown inland and the moon was out, glowing fiercely against the waters of the bay. The city was dark in the distance, and he could see the stars. He didn't used to be able to see them at night, not with the light pollution. It had only taken nuclear devastation to solve the problem.

"What are you doing up, Boss?"

He hadn't realized he'd moved until he found himself in a crouch behind a rusted-out dumpster, his Glock in his hand. Roach Mata watched him with amusement in her dark eyes, not even blinking at the gun being pointed at her.

"Damn it, Roach," he sighed, reholstering the pistol. "That's a good way to get yourself shot."

"It was worth it to watch you jump," she told him.

"I can't sleep and I didn't feel like drinking myself into a stupor," he answered her question honestly, then arched an eyebrow. "What's your excuse?"

"Too much shit on my mind," she said, shrugging, turning

away from him to look out over the bay. "Plus, it's pretty out tonight. It's usually so fucking ugly here."

"Night like this," he said, "you can almost forget what's happened. It almost looks normal."

She turned and eyed him sidelong, a confused, troubled look.

"You say shit like that, sometimes," she told him, "and I don't know what you mean. You can't be old enough to remember what it was like before, can you?"

He considered telling her the truth. He'd thought about it before. Roach he could almost trust. But how would she react? Would she stay if he told her what he was, or would she look at him like the freak he was? Was it worth the risk?

"My parents told me," he lied instead. "And I've seen movies, series from back then, same as you. This isn't normal." He waved a hand around them, at the shadowy husks of once-proud warships, at the blackened remains of buildings. "You don't have to be an old man to tell that. The way we live isn't the way things should be."

"It's how they are." Her tone wasn't so much argumentative as it was dejected. He was surprised. He'd never heard her like this. "It's how my parents grew up. My brothers and sisters, all my friends, this is how we live now, and all the shit you and Dix talk about, none of that seems real."

"You don't think we can get it back?" He realized he almost sounded hurt. He hadn't meant to, but he was afraid he was coming off as disappointed in her. "Do you not believe in what we're doing anymore?"

"What we're doing is fighting a holding action against an enemy who doesn't even know why *they're* here anymore, Boss." She shook her head. "It's worth doing, worth it to reduce the suffering they cause when they try to knock over what's left. But I don't think we're ever going to have what your parents or my grandparents had. Neither one of us is going to live long enough to see the United States they remember."

He glanced at her sharply, struck by the sudden, paranoid suspicion that she knew about him, but then he relaxed, realizing what she meant. She must have taken it as a sign he was upset about what she'd said, because she put a hand on his arm, apologetic.

"I know it means a lot to you, and to Dix, too. You were both in the military and the rest of us never were. But we have to understand what we're really doing here. We're trying to put out a forest fire with a plastic beach shovel."

"You've been thinking about this a lot," he realized. "Is that why you were so close to the edge today with Patty?"

She let her fingers slip off his forearm and there was a curious warmth left behind on his skin, a longing for human contact he hadn't realized he still possessed.

"Patty is an asshole." She shrugged diffidently. "That's probably all he is, but I don't trust him to have my back, not the way I trust the rest of you. He's only in this for the money, and once someone proves they can be bought, it's just a question of who's paying the most." She rolled her shoulders, tilting her head back and working the kinks out of her neck. "But yeah, it's been bugging me."

"We still have to work with him," Nate pointed out. "Is there any way you could make peace with him? It could just be he feels isolated out here." He snorted. "I mean, don't we all?"

She rolled her eyes, not hiding the disgust she felt, but finally she nodded, throwing her hands up in surrender.

"Fine. I'll talk to him tomorrow morning while Dix is working on the Tagan. But I can't promise I won't put my damned fist through that stupid dog-in-a-manger face of his if he starts smarting off at me again."

Nate grinned. It was a shame Roach was so much younger than him... *No, dumbass, she's fifteen years older than you are.*

"Well, I would order you to be nice to him," he said, "but a good officer never gives an order he knows won't be followed."

Geoff Patterson winced when he saw Rachel Mata walking toward him and turned back to the innards of his mech, trying to ignore her. The mech was simple, its demands understandable and easily met. It had grit and sand in the left hip actuator and all he had to do was clean it out. People were so much harder to figure.

He brushed vigorously at the joint with the stiff-bristled cleaner, focusing on his work and studiously ignoring everything else, until his arm was sore and the metal of the actuator housing was polished a bright silver. He paused to wipe the mid-morning sweat out of his eyes and finally saw Roach standing, watching him with crossed arms.

"Don't you got your own maintenance to do?" he asked her, setting the brush down on the tray beside the step-ladder.

"I'm surprised there's so much to clean up," she said archly. "I mean, it's not like you got into a fight or anything. Where'd you get all the damn sand from?"

"Jesus, Roach, can we not do this *again*?" he moaned, grabbing a rag to wipe the grease from his hands. "Don't we all got enough work to do?"

"I'm sorry," she said, surprising him. "I didn't mean to..." She waved a hand as if erasing the conversation. "Look, what I came over to say was, if there's something going on and you need help, I want to help. I know I can come on a little strong, but people shooting at you gets your blood pumping."

"No, I'm the one who's sorry," he told her, stepping down

the ladder, still a head taller than her but at least closer to eye-to-eye. "I screwed up and I nearly let you all get killed. I wasn't where I was supposed to be yesterday." He sucked in a breath, *wanting* to tell her all of it but knowing he couldn't. He *needed* to tell someone but he also wasn't suicidal. "We've had so many dry holes, so many false alarms, I didn't think anything would happen. I just thought I'd end up sitting in my mech, sweating my ass off for hours while you guys knocked over garbage dumpsters looking for imaginary Russians."

"So you flaked off?" she asked. It wasn't a chiding tone, instead almost...understanding?

"I found a nice beach somewhere and touched down," he admitted. "Somewhere with sand and not too much garbage, and no sewage in the water, and I got out and took off my boots and walked around in it."

"Jesus, where the hell is that?" she asked, eyes wide. "If there's no sewage, I want to go there!"

He chuckled. Roach was actually human, sometimes.

"Yorktown. Nobody goes there 'cause the bridge is out on one side and the roads are fucked up on the other. You can only reach it from the air, or by boat." He shrugged. "Or on foot, I guess."

"Shit, that's kind of close to the Quarantine Zone," she said, making a face like she'd bit into something sour. "You plan on having kids or do you just not care if they're born with webbed feet?"

"I didn't stay that long. Like I said, I wanted someplace with sand, even if it's radioactive." He closed his eyes, sighed. "It was just a few minutes, but it put me out of position when the call came in and I knew if I answered, you'd be able to figure out where I was. I did try to fly in, but it was all over before I was anywhere close."

"Tell me something, Patty, why are you out here? Is there really no other way to make money in Kentucky?"

"My family has bills," he told her, honestly this time. "Medical bills. I needed money fast or they were going to lose their home. I ain't really qualified for anything, but there was a government training program for the mechs…" He blinked at something in his eye, rubbed it away. "I miss my mom and my sisters sometimes. Ain't no way to call them, 'cause the connection out there isn't any good for anything but text."

"All right." There was a cast to her eyes as if he'd finally said something she could grab onto, some sort of common ground. "I tell you what, I know some people through my dad, and they have access to the government satellite communications net. If you want to set something up with your family, I can try to get them some screen time with you. Or if they're too far out, you can record some video here and I'll stream it to the government net and see if they can mirror it over to your family."

He smiled, and was shocked when he meant it.

"I'd like that. Thanks, Roach."

"No problem, man. Just keep me in the loop, okay?"

"Hey guys!" Ramirez called from the other side of the warehouse bay. Patty looked up and saw the man waving them toward the other end near the cargo doors, where they'd laid out the remains of the Tagan. "Dix has got into the CPU. Come check this shit out!"

Patterson deflated like a stuck balloon, as if the announcement had yanked him out of the good place he'd just been and back into the reality of the situation.

"Come on," Roach urged him. "You can help me explain to Mule why I'm not a 'guy.' Assuming you know the difference."

CHAPTER SIX_

"What's that Russian piece of shit got to tell us, Dix?" Nate asked between bites of his sandwich. It wasn't much, just pita bread, canned tuna and cheese. Regular bread went bad quick near the bay and you couldn't keep fresh meat around long, nor could you get it very often. The cheese was a treat, but it wouldn't last long, especially around Dix.

Dix didn't look up from the worktable where he had the Tagan's CPU cracked open, adaptor plugs jammed into its ports and back into his own tablet. He chewed on his lip, fingers holding open the alligator clips of a portable power supply, hovering over the motherboard as he tried to decide where to attach it.

"Don't know that I'd call it a piece of shit," Dix murmured, "since it was good enough to almost kill me."

Nate snorted, waving dismissively and taking a sip of energy drink, his fourth of the day. Massive doses of caffeine and sugar weren't any better for him than the ibuprofen or the cigarettes, but it kept him going.

"The thing surprised us," he said. "And that breaching

charge nearly took my Hellfire out before I even knew it was there. Not a fair fight."

"Jesus, Nate," Dix sighed. "You, more than anyone else here, should know that fair fights are for suckers."

"Preach it, Dix," Roach said, leaning back against the stand-up tool chest. "Hey, Ramirez, grab me a can of Rocket Juice, will you?"

"Your damn legs broken, Roach?" he griped, but did it anyway, walking over to the small refrigerator plugged into their generator and grabbing two cans of the energy drink, then shooting a questioning glance at Patty. "You want one while I'm over here?" he asked the tall man.

"Sure, thanks, Mule."

Ramirez scowled at the unwelcome nickname but picked out a third can anyway and carried them over to the other pilots.

"So whatcha got, Dix?" Roach asked the Navy pilot, popping open the can and taking a long swig, then belching with impressive volume and duration. Nate and Patty applauded with golf-claps and the woman took a small bow. "I'm missing my afternoon nap for this shit," she reminded him, going on as if there hadn't been an interruption.

"This shit ain't like hammering loose a stuck actuator *chica*," he told her archly over the top of the gimbal-mounted ring light/magnifying glass setup hanging between his eyes and the motherboard. "I fuck this up, we get nothing but a bunch of gibberish."

"Oh, don't give that shit," Roach teased him. "The damn computer software's doing all the heavy lifting, you're just plugging it in."

"So plug it in already, *viejito*," Ramirez urged him, laughing.

"Watch your mouth, Junior," Dix shot him a glare. "You're still the Mule so I ain't gotta take your lip."

Nate struggled to keep a straight face as Ramirez paled,

mouth dropping open. In the end, he couldn't do it and busted out in giggles just ahead of Dix and, amazingly, Patty.

"I'm just fucking with you, Mule," Dix said between guffaws, trying to hold onto the alligator clips even though his shoulders were shaking with laughter. "Now for real, all of you guys shut up for a second and let me concentrate."

He bit his lip again and attached the clips to a wire going into the Motherboard. The computer screen flashed to life with an hourglass symbol spinning in a three-dimensional starfield for a good ten seconds. Then folders and files began scrolling down the screen in Cyrillic, filling it up and scrolling downward faster than Nate could follow.

"Looks like you uncovered a shitload of Russian porn, Dix," Nate told him, wiping crumbs off his flight suit. The sandwich had been bland, but he'd still polished it off quickly. "If you find any redheads in there, you save those for me, all right?"

He felt as if the load on his shoulders had lightened a bit with Roach and Dix no longer at Patty's throat. Keeping everyone in a good mood was a challenge, especially in Norfolk...or hell, anywhere on the Eastern Seaboard.

Maybe we can finish this mission and get the fuck out of here soon, someplace not quite as scuzzy.

"I'm getting the program to translate," Dix told him, switching off the ring light and turning his attention to the display. "It'll do a keyword search, too, which should get us the GPS data and the communications log."

"And what's that gonna tell us?" Patty asked him. The Kentuckian seemed a bit subdued, quiet, and he wondered if Roach had talked to him.

"At the bare minimum, where the control rig for the Tagan was sitting, and where the mech flew in from." Dix shrugged. "Maybe where it's travelled for however long it's been since they reset the GPS recorder."

"That could be valuable if they smuggled it in," Roach said, nodding. "We might find out where they're using as a port."

"Ah, here we go." Dix slapped a palm on the table in triumph as information began to scroll across the screen in English. "There's the communications log, and the GPS data. Huh." He looked up and met Nate's eyes. "The fuckers were controlling it from a satellite this time."

"Do the Russians *have* any satellites up, still?" Ramirez wondered. "I thought I read somewhere we took their birds down early in the war."

"You *read?*" Roach asked him, eyes wide with disbelief.

"Oh, fuck you," Ramirez snapped, waving a hand at her impatiently.

"Maybe they did, maybe they didn't," Dix allowed, "but this is one of *our* birds. The control signal bounced off it, but it left an address."

"Well, don't keep us in suspense, Dix," Nate said, leaning forward on his elbows on the worktable.

Langley." He nodded out the open rear freight doors where the water was visible. "Right across the damned bay from us."

"The fuck?" Nate blurted. He paced over to the open bay doors, leaning with his hand against the edge of the doorway to look out over the Chesapeake as if he could see their enemies with the naked eye. "How the hell did they manage that? You got an Air Force base over there, along with what's left of the CIA headquarters, and even if some of the buildings got toasted, I know for a fact they can still do some serious signal intercept. How could they not detect a bunch of Russians in a van with a satellite transmission antenna in broad daylight?"

"Who says they were in a van?" Roach asked. Her lip curled in a sneer. "I've never trusted the spooks. You always read about them being arrested for selling out to the Russians or the Chinese. How much you wanna bet the Russians had someone in SatComs operate this thing for them?" She nodded towards the charred husk of the Tagan hanging from a cargo hook in a corner.

"Well, *that* ain't in here," Dix admitted. "But I'll tell you what is: we got the GPS data for where this Russian hunk of junk has been for the last three weeks."

Nate stalked back over to the worktable, leaning over Dix's shoulder to read the display. A map of Virginia and her adjoining states was laid out over the GPS readings, their track a red line ending at the pier where they'd destroyed the Tagan, trailing up a railroad line north up the coast and ending up in Maryland.

"Fucking Baltimore," Nate muttered. "No surprise there."

Baltimore was a nightmare, even before the nukes. You could smuggle just about anything in there as long as you were willing to risk getting killed for it.

"Where does that all leave us?" Roach demanded. "What do we know now we didn't before?"

Nate wanted to chide Roach for being too negative, but it was a damned good question. The CPU hadn't yielded anything useful except...

"Maybe that's how they found us," he speculated quietly. "If someone in Langley, either at the Air Base or the CIA, sold out to the Russians, they could have told them where we were operating."

Dix's eyes went wide and Roach began glancing around at the walls as if she expected them to close in on her.

"If that's so," Dix said, "then they might know where we..."

The alarm was one Nate had never expected to hear, the warbling staccato of the threat radar alerting them of incoming aircraft. For a moment, all of them were frozen, as if this were some shared nightmare they expected to wake up from at any second. Dix broke the paralysis, kicking away from his folding chair and lunging for the radar screen set up on a rolling table beside the bay doors. Nate was right on his heels, shamed into motion, knowing he should have been the first to act.

"What is it?" he asked, squinting at the mid-day haze. Even if there hadn't been a semi-permanent layer of pollution hanging over Norfolk, it would have been hard to make out anything in the harsh light.

"I'm seeing four bogies here," Dix reported, sounding much calmer than Nate. "Maybe...five klicks out, coming from the northeast. Moving slow, maybe a hundred knots."

"Translation for those of us who were never swabbies?" Roach asked.

"195 klicks an hour," Dix told her. "About 120 miles an hour for our undereducated Kentucky types," he added to Patty. He shrugged. "I mean, I ain't exactly air traffic control here, it could be helicopters."

"Everyone to their mechs," Nate decided, motioning towards the machines resting in their berth along the far wall. "If it's a false alarm, we'll all just be uncomfortable for a while, but I don't want to get caught with our thumbs up our ass."

Ramirez was closest and he was already halfway into his Hellfire before Patty and Roach even had their canopies open. Nate hung back for too long, eyes glued to the radar screen, barely noticing Dix running past him. From the four slow-moving aircraft there emerged four smaller blips, much faster and coming straight for them.

"Missiles!" he yelled, lunging across the room, knowing in his gut he had to get into his mech and knowing just as certainly he wasn't going to make it.

There was a distant hiss of rockets and a feeling at the back of his neck, static electricity raising the hackles, and some small part of his brain that was thinking rationally and not blanking out with fear remembered the ECM shield. It activated automatically when the radar detected incoming missile fire, nothing as fancy as a real military base would have had back in the day, no counter-missile batteries, no CWIS turrets. It was as basic as a pair of sounding rockets, launched in tandem and trailing a superconductive net into a protective arc, then triggering a charge through it when it reached a certain altitude.

He kept running, knowing what would happen when the missiles hit the net and their warheads detonated a couple hundred meters away. The magnetic field of the net would stop the fragmentation, but nothing was going to stop the...

Concussion!

The hand of God touched him and not in a loving way. Computers, repair equipment, the generator, the refrigerator and the wrecked Tagan spun and tumbled and fell and so did he. Concrete thumped him in the middle of the back, driving the breath out of his lungs, and the back of his head glanced against the floor despite an instinctive tuck of his chin, learned by his Prime in another life's jujitsu lessons. Flashes of light swam across his eyes and a moment's lethargy kept him from moving even though he knew he had to get up or die.

Hands were yanking him to his feet and pushing him towards his mech and he knew it was Dix. He wanted to tell the man to leave him, to get to his own machine because there wasn't enough time. The enemy would be here in seconds and it was taking too long, but talking would take even longer and it would be a waste of time because he wouldn't listen anyway.

Glimpses of the carnage around him like film frames between the flashes of pain and stars in his vision. Patty and Ramirez were locked in, powered up, their Hellfires pulling away from their maintenance racks, Patty knocking half of his over with reckless speed. Roach was pulling herself into her seat, her legs kicking as she struggled upward through the cockpit hatch.

And a Tagan was hovering outside the open loading bay, its chain gun tracking toward them.

"Dix, get down!" he tried to yell at his friend, but by then it was far too late, the words swallowed up in the full-throated roar of the 25mm firing.

Blood splashed across Nate's face, a sticky, metallic taste in his mouth and a wash of red stinging his eyes, blinding him. He spat and wiped at his eyes, wondering if he'd get the chance to see the round that killed him. What he saw instead was Patty rocketing across the warehouse, jets screaming, Vulcan spitting fire. The Tagan vectored its thrusters forward, braking frantically against its forward momentum as the 20mm rounds punched through its chest armor.

Patty roared off after it with Ramirez rushing unto the breach just behind him, high-tech knights charging into battle.

Dix. Where's Dix? Jesus, there's blood all over me...

There wasn't much left of Lieutenant Bryan Richardson, and what was there was nearly unrecognizable as having once been a living, breathing human. There were bits of him, like a raccoon in the highway, hit by a truck and scattered over the road until you couldn't tell one part from another. Nate wanted to throw up, wanted to bury his head in his hands and surrender to the inevitable, but somehow Roach was there.

She'd climbed out of her mech and she was yelling something at him, but his ears were too battered to understand for a moment.

"Nate!" she was saying. "You have to mount up! We have to help them!"

His guys. He had to help his guys. He nodded furtively and clambered up into the cockpit of his mech, his motions mechanical, brain turned onto autopilot. He shut out the visions he knew he'd see when he tried to sleep, the smells and the taste, the feeling of the blood soaking his flight suit to his skin. He shut out the feelings, the disgust and the fear and the shock and concentrated on the job, on the duty.

Take the fight to the enemy. Get them before they get us. The thoughts were his, but he heard them in Dix's voice. *We're BAMF, Nate,* he'd always say, *Bad Ass Mother Fuckers. Let's show them.*

CHAPTER SEVEN_

Thrust pushed Nathan Stout back into his seat, the pressure seeming to grind Dix's blood into his skin, a tribal tattoo from some savage ritual. Dix had tried to talk the whole team into getting matching tattoos once, the unit patch on their right forearms, but Patty hadn't wanted to let some unlicensed back-room artist give him Hepatitis with unsterilized needles and Roach had, surprisingly enough, said it was against her religion, though she wouldn't specify which religion that was.

Apparently, her religion doesn't have any problem with killing, he thought, watching her Hellfire jet past his on shimmering columns of heat distortion, Mark-Ex missiles streaking away from her launch pod.

It was just the four of them against the four Tagans...there hadn't been time to link up with the U-mechs they had left after the battle. He didn't know for sure if any of the Tagans were unpiloted, but something about the way they were moving said no. They were too independent of each other, none of them mirroring the others, each taking on their Hellfires individually.

Well, except two of them were coming after Patty, from separate angles, trying to take him out before Nate and Roach could get into the fight. Nate started to target one of them with a Mark-Ex until he remembered his launch pod was empty, drained in the fight earlier. *None* of them had re-armed with missiles---it was standard procedure not to leave them loaded while in the base---and he couldn't remember if everyone had even topped off the hoppers of their Vulcans.

He hadn't. His 20mm was dry.

They caught us napping, flat-footed. It's my fault, but my people are going to pay for it.

He switched to his twin 40mm cannons, but that was a forlorn hope, designed for use against vehicles and dismounted infantry, not nearly enough to penetrate the heavy armor on a Tagan.

Maybe enough to distract them, though.

He boosted towards Patty, angling in behind one of the pair of enemy mechs firing at the Kentucky pilot. The chain gun's tracers were a science fiction movie laser gun cutting red slashes across the muddy sky, most of the slow, heavy slugs missing but one smacking into Patty's shoulder in a shower of sparks. Patty spun away from the fire, still trying to keep the other Tagan in his sights, firing off bursts from his Vulcan.

Nate set his targeting reticle over the Russian mech directly ahead of him, toggled the weapons control to the forties and squeezed the trigger. The thud-thud-thud of their reports were the hollow footsteps of a giant on a wooden floor, infuriatingly slow and useless, but it was all he had. The rounds themselves were so slow he could see them in flight, black dots against the haze, but the splashes of roiling fire they produced when they struck the Tagan's rear armor were visually satisfying.

And a light show was all they produced. That and a distraction. The Tagan spun in mid-air and came after Nate, as if it were a bull and he'd just waved a red cape.

Be careful what you wish for.

Nate was already turning when the Tagan launched his missile. He couldn't outrun it, not in a mech with a top speed of just over a hundred miles an hour, so he dove straight down. There was nothing beneath them but the Chesapeake Bay…and the bare bones of an old Navy destroyer. He didn't know her name, though he supposed he could have looked it up if he'd been of a mind. It hadn't seemed important, just one of those details from the past the technicians had decided to omit from his memory.

It was important to him now, whatever its name had been. He was low over the water now, spraying sheets of it in his wake as he curved around the bow of the rusted and charred hulk, dragging the missile behind him. He felt its detonation more than he heard it, a gong thundering through the superstructure of the destroyer on the port side while he rounded the starboard. He fed power to the thrusters, mindful of the heat readings flashing yellow at him in the display, telling him he was pushing the stress limits of the turbines to the bitter edge. He took them just high enough to get him over the prow of the ship, then he set down on the deck and waited for the enemy to catch up.

The Tagan didn't bother with another missile, maybe because he figured Nate's anti-missile machine guns would have too good a chance of intercepting it with him standing on solid ground, or maybe because his own jets were beginning to overheat. It was the natural limitation of a mech—lifting something so heavy and unaerodynamic required a lot of power, which the isotope reactors could produce, but also a lot of thrust, which overtaxed the best turbines anyone knew how to make.

Mechs could fly, but they couldn't fly very far, or very fast, or for very long. The main advantage they had was versatility. They combined the firepower and maneuverability of an attack helicopter with the armor of a tank and they only took one pilot to fly, plus they could serve as a control center for U-mechs, which had the same advantages as well as serving as armed drones.

Sometimes, though, Nate wondered if the military had just adapted them because they looked so damned cool. He cut loose again with the forties and the Tagan dodged, even though no individual round would have hurt him, an instinctive sort of move. Nate took advantage of his distraction and ran, footpads digging into the rusted deck of the old ship as he tried to put the fore superstructure of the old, pre-stealth design between him and the enemy. Chain gun rounds chased him, blowing fist-sized holes through the ancient steel in even rows but not quite penetrating far enough to come out the other side when he ducked down for cover.

This is the damnedest game of tag I've ever played.

The Tagan chased, staying grounded for now. Nate could have taken off again—the heat sensors had sunken down into the green range again—but he wasn't trying to lose the enemy mech. He wanted to keep it interested in him, keep it off Patty's ass, give the others a chance at a one-on-one fight.

The Hellfire's footsteps on the deck were Lambeg drums sounding in some ancient battle in the Scottish Highlands, dramatic and thundering, but all Nate could do was whisper a half-hearted prayer that the thin metal would hold under his weight. Falling through to a lower deck probably wouldn't be fatal in and of itself, not inside the Hellfire, but it would let the Tagan get back into the fight with the others. He passed the smoke funnel and the broken, jagged remains of the aft mass, but before he could reach the aft superstructure, a double-tap of 25mm rounds blew his 40mm cannons off their mount.

The rending screech of ripping metal set his teeth on edge and the mech yawed to the right with the loss of the weight. Even if he hadn't known his mech as well as his own body, even if he hadn't been able to read the damage indicators in his

HUD, the damn guns went spinning right across the front of his canopy, taunting him with the loss of his last meaningful weapon.

Got to keep moving, he chided himself, shoving the mech forward, regaining balance through brute force, pounding the machine's footpads into the deck so hard he felt it buckle slightly beneath them.

The aft superstructure was a crumbling ruin, but it was still tall enough to give him cover from the guns of the Tagan...and, more importantly, block the enemy's thermal scans. He clomped to a halt so abruptly his restraints bit into his chest and the breath wheezed out of him. He pivoted in place and stomped down on the controls for the thrusters. The jets lifted the Hellfire ten meters into the air, still just beneath the upper edge of the aft superstructure, and beneath him, the Tagan rushed around the corner.

Nate cut power to the jets and left his stomach somewhere near the top of the superstructure while the rest of him plunged downward, directly onto the back of the hunched-over Tagan. He'd bit down on his mouthpiece at the last second and without it, he would have bitten clean through his tongue or broken every tooth out of his head when the impact came. The jolt through the hips and into the torso of the Hellfire felt as if it wanted to drive his spine up through his skull but the mech's knees gave, bending as the footpad pistoned into the Tagan's turbine housings, smashing them inward, crumpling them like cardboard. And driving the enemy mech right over the side of the destroyer.

Nate hit his thrusters at the very last second, hovering just over the side of the destroyer for a moment before he set the Hellfire back down on the deck and watched the Tagan hit the water.

If the Tagan's jets had been operational, he could have gone a hundred meters down and still made it back up again---the isotope reactor could heat up anything and pump it through the jets, including water. Hell, he'd even heard they'd taken Hellfires up into space early in the war, before everything had gone to shit, and ran the jets off external tanks of reaction mass.

Without the jets, the Tagan was several tons of dead weight heading on a one-way trip to the bottom of the bay. Nate winced. It was a bad way to go. His expression flattened out when he thought of Dix. There were no good ways to go in this business.

He hurt everywhere twice over, felt like someone had worked him over with a baseball bat and then run him over with a car to finish the job, but there was still work to do. He hit the thrusters and lifted back into the fight, trying to get a fix on where the rest of the team was. Their IFF transponders flashed blue in his HUD as he lifted above the interference of all the metal in the old destroyer and spun his mech slowly around, painting a picture of the battle.

Roach was on the ground, back at the pier and still in motion, her damage control reports still nominal. The woman was one hell of a pilot, especially for someone without real military experience. The Tagan she'd been dogfighting wasn't in nearly as good a shape, if the thermal readings were to believed, and she didn't seem as if she needed any help.

Patty was nearly three kilometers away from the warehouse, running hot at just over a hundred meters over the water, launching what the readings said was his last Mark-Ex missile at an enemy machine trying to hug the waves below him. The strategy didn't work and the Tagan disappeared in a devouring gout of white flame and black smoke.

Ramirez was closest to Nate's position over the destroyer and not doing nearly as well. Mule was on the run, arcing around the perimeter of the bay, his jets nearing the redline and damage indicators flashing a solid yellow almost everywhere. He was Winchester on missiles and Vulcan ammo and he'd started with a full combat load.

Damn it, that's what happens when you send a Mule into a fight without someone holding his hand.

"Patty, help me out," he called to the tall Kentuckian. "Mule's in trouble!"

Nate didn't wait to see if the man obeyed, just kicked his Hellfire in the pants and set up an intercept course. What he was going to do once he got there he hadn't quite figured out, since he was pretty much unarmed.

Details, he heard Dix's voice in his head snorting a laugh. *We figure that shit out on the fly, Nate.*

Pain clutched at his chest and he wasn't sure if it was grief or incipient cracked ribs. Either way, he was going to pay for it later.

He tried to come up with a plan, estimating where the Tagan would be at his intercept point, where Patty would be, where Ramirez would be, and suddenly the math and the physics just clicked inside his head and he knew what to do.

"Ramirez," he called. "Set your ass down and get to cover, right now!"

Mule didn't answer, but he feathered his port jet and descended in a tight spiral, touching down with his mech's legs already working like some cartoon character. The Tagan adjusted course to follow, putting itself right where Nate wanted it.

"I'm out of missiles, Boss," Patty warned him. "And I'm damned close to Winchester on twenty mike-mike, too."

"You got a fist, don't you?" Nate demanded, sounding a bit shorter with the man than he'd intended just because of the aching in his chest. And knees. And shoulders. "You aren't out of those, right?"

"I got you. Roger that, Boss."

The Tagan was lining up on Ramirez, bobbing back and forth in its flight and firing off short bursts of 25mm as it tried to get a bead on him. Mule was scrambling across the soft sand of the beach beside the pier, limping badly on his mech's left leg, trying to find something to hide behind and not having much success. It probably wouldn't matter.

The Tagan pilot noticed him when he was about three hundred meters away and spun in mid-air, braking to face him. The enemy mech fired wildly but Nate cut power and sank below the red streaks of the incoming tracers, below the firing arc of the chain gun, reaching up with his mech's articulated left hand just as he was about to pass below the feet of the Tagan. The claws of the hand caught the gun mount of the enemy mech's and Nate cut power to the jets completely, yanking down on the chain gun with the full weight of the Hellfire. The weapon tore away from the mech's right arm, the feed drums ripping away and spilling glittering brass cartridges out of the sky.

Nate was falling and he goosed the turbines desperately, pushed down into his seat by a gush of power from the jets. He didn't look at the ground rushing up at him, kept his eyes upward where Patty was cruising in at seventy miles an hour. He nearly missed off to the right, swinging his left claw in a wide, arcing strike. It hammered into the cockpit of the Tagan, shattering polymer and crushing metal and terminating against something solid enough to send him coasting backward before he corrected with his thrusters.

The Tagan drifted away as well, but made no move to change its course because its pilot upper torso was a red smear splattered over what was left of the cockpit. The mech's jets sputtered as pressure came off the throttle and it began to drop, gradually at first but with gathering speed. The sickening crunch of metal reached Nate even through the cockpit. Ramirez stopped trying to hide behind an inadequate garbage dumpster and peeked out around it.

Nate touched down near the wreckage, finally letting himself relax...and immediately started to shake. He grabbed at the steering yokes, clenched them tightly until he'd regained control of himself. For the moment.

Patty had landed beside him and his Hellfire stood motionless, arms held away from the torso like a bodybuilder who couldn't completely relax because of the size of his pecs. He said nothing and Nate couldn't see his face from the reflection of the noonday sun on his canopy. He wanted to ask if the man was okay, but he had to check on Mata first.

"Roach, you okay?" He could see her icon on the IFF and she was moving along the shoreline just down from the warehouse pier. He didn't see any sign of the Tagan she'd been fighting on his radar, lidar or thermal.

"I'm good." The reply came immediately, but her voice was flat, listless and he worried she'd been injured.

"Mata, report," he snapped the order crisply, trying to shock her into a complete reply.

"I destroyed the enemy mech, sir," she said, an edge of anger in her tone. "No damage to my Hellfire. I am currently on foot to allow my turbines to cool down."

"Roger," he acknowledged. "Meet us back at the warehouse." He switched to the general net to include Patty and Ramirez. "Everybody needs to head to base right now. We need to get out shit on a barge and get the hell out of here. They know where we are and God knows when they'll be back."

No one replied and he fought back irritation. He understood the lethargy, the unwillingness to accept the reality. He felt it himself. But they needed to move while they still had time.

"Technician Ramirez, Sergeant Patterson," he said, an edge to the words, "I am going to need a voice response."

"Yes, sir," Ramirez said instantly with the tone of embarrassment the new guy always had when he thought he'd screwed up.

Patty waited a beat, almost challenging, but finally he murmured, "I hear you," and hit his jets.

Nate waited until he was sure Ramirez and Roach had followed Patty before he finally gave himself a moment to let go, to relax his grip. His body shuddered, racked with sobs that seemed to come out of nowhere, the tears streaming down his face uncontrolled. He gave it a full minute, let the grief pass through and have its way, felt it flow through him and out of him.

It was quick, a morning squall.

It had to be. He didn't have the time for anything more.

CHAPTER EIGHT_

Geoff Patterson wiped his chin and spat out what was left of the vomit. It splattered across the sink and onto the bathroom floor, but he made no move to clean it up. They were evaccing the warehouse anyway.

Maybe when the Russians come back to check on it, they'll clean it up for me. They fucking owe me that much.

There wasn't even any water to rinse his mouth out. This place had no running water, at least none you wanted to drink, and they'd already hauled everything useful out onto the barge —spare parts, ammo, all the repair equipment including what had been busted in the attack, cargo cranes, personal gear, everything.

Everything except what was left of Dix's body. Nate had pushed the remains together with a broom and covered the bloody mess with a tarp before they'd started working. Patty and the others had stayed in their mechs as long as they could, loading gear requiring the strength of the machines while Nate had recovered what needed a gentler touch. But then the time had come to store the Hellfires on the barge and get ready to go.

"I need a volunteer," Nate had said, his face so carefully neutral. "I need someone to help me bring Dix on board."

And for some damned reason, Patty had stepped forward. Guilty conscience, maybe. But he hadn't been able to do it. They'd intended to wrap Dix's remains in the tarp and carry it onto the barge like that, but all it had taken was a hand slipping out, slapping wet against the concrete for Patty to lose it. He'd barely made it to the doorway before he puked the first time. It hadn't been the last and he'd retreated to the bathroom to get away from the others. He didn't want them to see him because he was afraid they'd know. He was afraid they'd see the guilt.

He was glad someone had taken the bathroom's mirror. He didn't want to look himself in the face.

"Patty?"

It was Roach. She didn't knock because the only door was an old shower curtain, so moldy and tattered they hadn't even bothered to retrieve it. He stayed silent, hunched over the sink, hoping she'd go away.

"Patty, are you okay?" she persisted. "Look, none of us blame you."

You would, if you knew, he told her silently.

"Hell, I almost threw up myself and the only reason Mule didn't was he puked in his mech during the fight and there wasn't anything left." She didn't even chuckle at her own attempt at lightening the mood. "We got to go now, though. The barge is about to pull out. Nate wants you to come on out."

I should stay here. If I stay here, they won't know where to find you. You'll be safe from me.

He wanted to say that, but instead he spat one last time and pulled the curtain aside. Roach waited for him, arms crossed over her breasts like she wasn't sure what to do with her hands. She looked lost, like she didn't want to be there but was doing it anyway because it was her duty. Roach was all about duty.

He walked past her, past the shower curtain walls hanging in sad, molding memorial to their time in the warehouse. Out on the shop floor, where the mechs had stood, there was nothing but a pile of trash spilled out of a plastic can during the attack. And the blood. The blood was still there, clotting and drying. In a few weeks, it would be just another stain on the concrete, another story no one would be around to tell.

"Did Dix have any family?" Patty asked Roach, hesitating before he passed through the doorway. "Kids? Parents? Anything?"

"If he did, I never heard him talk about them," she admitted, eyes flickering outward, upward, looking everywhere but at the blood. "All he ever talked about was his time in the Navy, like it was the only part of his life that mattered."

Probably divorced, Patty thought. *Marriage couldn't survive him being away all the time. Or maybe she died in the war. Lots of people from here in the East have family who died in the war.*

Nate and Ramirez were on the barge, waiting. Ramirez had an M37 carbine at his shoulder, eyes scanning the horizon as if he were some sort of fierce sentinel, as if the 6.5mm popgun would do a damned thing against a Tagan if the Russians sent more of them. The Hellfires were all strapped onto the deck, along with the other gear, covered with tarps to conceal its nature from random looters.

"Hurry up, you two," Nate urged them, his beat-up old Glock in his hand. "I want to be at the new location before it gets dark."

Which was going to be in another hour or two—the sun was low in the sky, obscured by haze.

Roach hopped onto the barge obediently, grabbing a rifle from where it leaned against a tarp-covered case of 20mm ammo and taking up a guard position.

Always the loyal bitch.

"I'm not going." He heard himself saying it, but he didn't remember making the decision.

Nate frowned at him. The old man always tried to look so serious, but Patty thought he just looked constipated, like there was a stick stuck up his ass, holding everything in.

"Patty, we're all upset right now, but..."

"I said I'm not going," he insisted. "I can't. Not with..." He nodded toward the tarp at the bow of the barge, wrapped tight but still leaking blood at one end. The sight of it made him want to throw up food he hadn't eaten yet.

Nate squeezed his eyes shut, rubbing his fingers over them like he had a headache. Patty braced himself for an argument, but the man surprised him by nodding. He leaned over and picked up one of the M37's and tossed it underhanded. Patty caught it, slung the weapon over his shoulder.

"Meet us at the old Coast Guard station at Portsmouth," Nate told him. "You can take one of the trucks." He motioned to the other side of the warehouse. Patty couldn't see the parking lot from here, but he knew the two old pickups were still out there, salvaged from an impound lot and repaired for short-range jaunts. "It'll be more dangerous going overland," Nate warned.

"I'll meet you there," Patty said.

"We're having a memorial for Dix tonight. 2200 hours. Don't be late."

Patty nodded, saying nothing, watching them as they cast off from the dock. The barge's electric motors hummed in near silence, drowned out by the gurgling of churned water from the propellers, and the heavy, flat-top boat threaded its way through the wreckage of ancient dreams and out into the bay.

When it was gone from sight, Patty walked to the old Ford and opened the passenger's side, tossing the rifle into the seat. The upholstery was ripped and faded, the windows cracked. At the driver's side, he hesitated, looking out at the pothole-strewn road away from the docks.

I should just get on it and start driving, he told himself. *Just not stop till I'm back in Kentucky.*

He snorted, sliding behind the wheel.

And then what? Be right back where you started? Would Mom be happy to see you come back without the money you promised?

He imagined her pinched, wrinkled face glaring at him with that patented look of disapproval she'd perfected when his father had still been around. It would serve her right if he never came back, just let her rot there with the rest of his worthless, drug-cooking relatives.

Sheeit, he sighed, sliding into the driver's seat and cranking the engine. *If you were gonna do that, you'd never have come out here in the first place.*

He pulled out onto the road. Wherever it led, he would have to see it through.

The desk, Nathan Stout reflected, was probably as old as the base. It was faded, puke-green metal gnawed on by rust, and one of the legs had bent in, but it weighed at least a hundred kilos and no one had bothered to salvage or steal it in the decades it had been squatting in its lair, ruling what was left of the Coast Guard base. He imagined some officious Chief Petty Officer ruling this office like a minor noble from behind his fortress of a desk, trying to decide how he could best make the lives of his or her troops more complicated.

The rest of the office had been bare, the walls peeled and cracked, but there'd been plenty of room for his cot and personal gear. There were no windows, which was just as well, since it meant the rain hadn't gotten in and made the walls moldy, but it was going to get damned stuffy in here during the day and the portable lamps providing the only light gave everything an orange tint. He'd found a loose brick near a collapsed wall outside and it propped up the broken leg nicely. His folding chair went behind the desk and he leaned on its flat, expansive surface, remembering more stable days, closer to normal, where most of a military career was lived behind such desks and ninety percent of the soldiers and sailors and airmen and marines never heard a shot fired in anger.

That it was someone else's memories didn't seem to matter to him this time.

He had nothing to put in the desk drawers, though. No one used paper for much anymore, which was a good thing since there was no one left producing or shipping it anymore either. He remembered paper reports, paper notebooks, physical books you could read. You still saw those laying around in old libraries and book stores, at least where people hadn't used them to feed their fires in the winter. He had a couple himself, for old time's sake, despite the thousands of books he kept on his phone.

The Prime had dim memories of a time before people could read books and watch movies and take videos with their phones, a time when phones were just for talking. He'd been a young boy then, but it had stuck with him and, for some reason, a residue of the memory had been passed along to his dupes. Maybe it had a connection to something the DoD techs had considered important.

He stumbled on another residual memory and smiled sadly. Well, yeah, there was one thing he could put in the desk. He scooted his chair back and went to his duffle bag, the one with his name stenciled onto the side of it in black paint. He dug inside until he found the bundle wrapped in old T-shirts and pulled it out carefully. Inside was a bottle of Jack Daniels, the real stuff, not the homebrews they refilled old whiskey bottles with here in the East. He set it on the desktop, then unwrapped the two shot glasses he'd salvaged from a gift shop in DC a year ago.

They wore the Presidential seal, which he'd always found hilarious. The President hadn't been anywhere near DC in years. He was stuck in a bunker in Colorado along with what was left of the military, desperately trying to hold onto what was left, the slice of what had been America west of the Mississippi and just overlapping the Rocky Mountain states. The Russians had inroads into the Eastern Seaboard and controlled the Alaskan ports. The Chinese had moved into the Pacific Northwest, not that anybody in the US government cared. From what he'd heard, the Oregon and Washington State governments got along just fine with China.

California had split into three separate nations, all three of them constantly fighting each other, while Arizona, New Mexico and Nevada were wastelands with no water and whatever cities were left controlled by the drug cartels.

He sat back down, feeling the pain and exhaustion pulling him into the chair. He needed a cigarette, but his last pack had gotten burned up in the attack. He unscrewed the cap on the bottle of Jack and poured three fingers into each of the glasses, setting one in front of him and one across the desk as if for someone else.

"One last drink, Dix," he murmured, picking up his shot glass and toasting his absent friend. The whiskey was smooth, with a mule-kick at the end and he let the warmth of the shot burn inside his chest for a moment before he set the glass down.

He stared at the other glass, wondering if he should empty it on the ground or something symbolic like that. Instead, he picked it up and downed it, figuring Dix would be pissed if he wasted good whiskey like that. Then the bottle and the glasses went into the right bottom drawer and he pushed it shut.

"Where the fuck were you?"

He glanced at the closed office door. It was thick metal and not much got through it from the hallways outside, but Roach had a way of pitching her voice to penetrate any wall and she sounded pissed. He pushed himself up, feeling the desk shift slightly on its makeshift stand, and yanked the door open, feeling it stick where the frame had warped from years of neglect and lack of air conditioning.

Sound washed into the room through the open door, seeming to carry further in the darkened hallway than it would have during the day.

"You missed the fucking funeral!" Roach was still yelling. "You think Dix would have missed your service if it had been you that bought it?"

"I don't like funerals," Patty said, subdued and much more softly than anything Roach had said. "I think he'd have understood."

Nate followed the voices down the hall to the reception area. It was open to the night, the windows long shattered, but they'd hung mosquito netting across the vacant panes and done their best to clean out the accumulated leaves and detritus. An old table and a few ratty office chairs had been pulled into the room across from the front desk, and they'd hung lanterns from the unpowered cord for a chandelier, which gave everything a harsh, even light.

Patty stood wearing the same greasy, stained flight suit as he had after the battle, the rifle hanging from his shoulder. Roach was inches from his face, leaning in as she yelled, finger pointing like a weapon, while Ramirez hung back, hands on his hips, happy to let her do the dirty work.

"Not to mention you left us with all the work of moving our

shit in," Ramirez chimed in, apparently feeling emboldened. "You know how long that took, man?"

"I said I was sorry," Patty insisted.

"Where did you sleep last night?" Nate wondered.

Patty frowned at him as if he thought it was an odd thing to say. It was, Nate realized, a strange question for him to ask given all the other problems and worries Patty's absence had created the last day and a half, but it was the first that came to his mind, and he was too exhausted to filter his thoughts.

"In the truck," the tall man answered, haltingly, grudgingly. "I pulled it into a parking garage and got a few hours' sleep. I just needed some time to think."

"And did it help?"

"Could I talk to you in private?" Patty wondered.

Nate shrugged. "Sure. Give that rifle to Ramirez so he can stick it back with the others."

He didn't *really* believe Patty would get pissed off enough to shoot him, but he'd been wrong before.

Patty seemed to consider it for a moment, but he shrugged the sling off his shoulder and handed the M37 to Ramirez. It was a bulky weapon, mostly polymer, and a stray strand of memory reminded him it had once been produced by FN, a Belgian company back when there'd been a Belgium. They'd called it the SCAR-Heavy, which, he supposed, meant there'd once been a SCAR-Light, though he couldn't recall why one was heavy and one wasn't.

He filed it away in the dusty archives of useless knowledge and led Patty back into the office. The Kentuckian pushed the door shut behind them, then had to turn again and shove it closed against that fraction of a centimeter of warp.

"I'd tell you to sit down," Nate apologized, "but I only have the one chair so far."

He thought about offering Patty a drink, but decided against introducing alcohol to whatever volatile mood the younger man was in.

"It's okay," Patty said, shrugging it away. "I've been sitting in that damn truck for hours, anyway." His hands were stuffed into his pockets and he didn't seem to want to meet Nate's eyes. "Look, Boss, like I told them, I'm really sorry I missed the memorial. I was thinking about Dix my own way, you know? But I..." He tilted his head back and blew out a sigh. "All this has been making me think about my family. I'm out here in the shit trying to help them, but I'm starting to feel like I'll never see them again."

"We're all of us taking the same risk, Geoff."

"I know. But my initial contract is up in just two months." Patty finally looked him in the eye. "The one I signed to get the free training from the military. I'd like to get out of it early. The government would approve it if you signed off on it. I'd even promise to come back and finish it up if you want, after I go spend some time with my mom and family for a while."

Nate slowly and carefully leaned back on the edge of the desk and it shifted precariously on the brick stuck under the one broken stand. He was so damned tired.

"Patty, we're down to just the four of us now. We've got an active Russian military presence somewhere here in Norfolk and they've already killed one of us. The CIA and Army Intelligence doesn't know shit, or they aren't telling us shit, which is all one and the same as far as I'm concerned. And now you want to just take off? You think I can troll the local bars and find a replacement who's trained to fly a Hellfire?" He shook his head. "Jesus, I don't even know when or *if* I'll be able to find someone to replace Dix! Ramirez is the closest thing we have to a mechanic now, and he's just barely able to maintain the guns! What happens if we get a thruster damaged?"

"I know and I'm sorry about that," Patty said, and Nate was

pretty sure the man was grinding his teeth to keep himself under control. "But I need to see my family."

Nate rubbed a hand over his face, feeling sweat and grime accumulated over the last two days without a shower.

"Look, I'll tell you what. I'll put out a request through the DoD Contractor Recruitment Web for two new pilots. As soon as I get at least one, I can let you go. Until then, we're just stretched too thin." He spread his hands helplessly. "I'm afraid that's the best I can do."

Patty's face screwed up into a scowl and Nate thought for an instant he was in for a knock-down, drag-out argument, but then the man's shoulders sagged as if in surrender.

"You should go, too," Patty told him, eyes on the floor, fumbling for the door knob. "We all should. We should get out of here and leave this fucking worthless place to the Russians. I don't even know what the hell they want with it."

"We're all doing what we can to try to rebuild things the way they were," Nate protested, but it was mechanical, automatic, as if he were reading from a script. "If we let the Russians operate here without opposition, they'll strip all the resources they can and then move west and do it again and we'll just have to fight them there, or keep running until there's nowhere left. We have to take back the United States."

Patty turned back from the door, and now he didn't seem resigned or resentful anymore. He was angry.

"Nate, do you know where I live?"

"Kentucky."

"Frankfort. Do you know what it's like there? Do you know what it's like in the rest of Appalachia?"

"I've never been there," Nate admitted. Neither had the Prime, unless that was one of those unimportant discards.

"We get *nothing* from the federal government," Patty told him. "Not a damn thing. We barter for supplies and the corporate banks run everything, own all the land, all the businesses that still hire. You do what they say, you work for who they tell you to work or you don't fuckin' eat. And if you're sick and can't work and you miss a payment or two on your house, they rip it right out from under you, whether there's anyone else to sell it to or not. People starve to *death* out there, Nate." Patty's eyes were wide now, his nostril flaring, and Nate's right hand drifted toward the Glock still holstered at his right hip.

"They wander the streets begging for food," Patty went on, his voice intense but not raised. "They're fucking shadows, skeletons that everyone pretends not to see because no one has anything to spare. And then you find one of them dead in an alley and the cops come and take him away and bury him in an unmarked grave."

Patty snorted, yanking the door open. It shrieked in protest. "That's gonna be all of us, this whole country. We're all just shadows wandering in the streets, and someday we'll just fade away." He paused in the doorway, fixing Nate with a stare. "There's no going back. Not out here. If you want anything like your old America, you should go move to Kansas and hope reality doesn't catch up with you before you die."

Patty stalked out and Nate hesitated just a moment before he followed him. Roach was still out in the reception area, kicked back in a folding lawn chair they'd scraped up from some abandoned house months ago, while Ramirez was just coming back from the armory. Patty started to stride past them, but Nate spoke up, stopping him.

"Wait," he said. Patty turned back and Ramirez and Roach looked up at him expectantly. "Look, I know we all got a lot on our plate, trying to find the Russians and with what happened to Dix, but..." He shrugged. "We aren't going to accomplish anything until we get our heads right."

"What'd you have in mind, Boss?" Roach asked him.

"We're living in each other's laps here. We need to get out of here and cut loose a little."

"You mean into town?" Ramirez asked, eyes going wide. "But that's..."

"Against regs?" Nate shrugged. "Sure. But I'd rather risk a fine from the DoD than everyone going nuts and killing each other." He motioned to Ramirez. "Go set the alarms and lock everything down. Change out of your flight suits and get a shower. We leave in an hour."

CHAPTER NINE_

Granby Street used to be a happening place, or so Nate had been told. He remembered reading that the NorVa performing arts center had been voted one of the top venues in the United States fifty years ago or so. Now it was a crumbling heap of bricks and wood, half of it burned to ash in the fires after the nuclear attack.

What would it be like, he wondered, to go to a concert with tens of thousands of people? To crowd into an auditorium like that and not be afraid of a terrorist bombing or an enemy attack? He couldn't imagine it.

"This place is a little depressing," Roach murmured aside to him, keeping her voice low enough the others probably couldn't hear it over the hollow sounds of their own footsteps on the deserted street.

"It's better once you get to the Fry," he said, shrugging it off.

"If you like drug dealers and hookers."

He eyed her sidelong. "You think it was a bad idea coming here?"

"Naw, the boys needed it." She nodded toward Ramirez and Patty, who were shoulder to shoulder, speaking in low tones about something Nate couldn't make out. "Especially Patty. He's about to pop a cork."

"He wants out of his contract," Nate confided. At her look of shock, he put a finger over his lips. "Keep it to yourself. But yeah, he's missing his family big-time, I guess."

"Shit." She shook her head. "How the hell would we replace him?"

"Well, we fucking can't right now," he declared, snorting as if it were obvious. "I told him I'd put a request into the DoD contractor procurement web, but how fast do you think they're going to get back with us?"

"I know you got Ramirez and me through Dix's connections," she said. "Was Patty from the procurement system?"

"He was," Nate confirmed. "And I put the request in a solid *year* before he showed up."

Bright lights shone and loud music carried around the next corner, signaling their arrival at the Fry. Nate didn't know where the name had come from, but he knew it had been postwar. He'd heard various explanations for it, from the idea that it originated with the food carts offering fried rat to the more appetizing if also more depressing possibility that it was named for the charring of the taller buildings from the edges of the flash of the nuke at the harbor.

Either way, the Fry had grown from a few food carts to what passed for a night life in postwar Richmond. The buildings were mostly unsafe still, which meant only employees went inside to bring out stores or cook food, while customers and sound equipment and a few surprisingly talented live bands huddled under tarps stretched over the street, hung with mosquito netting because the portable lights sure as hell attracted them. Nate slapped at one on his neck and grimaced as his hand came away with a stain of red on the palm. He picked up his pace, pulling even with Patty and Ramirez.

"First round's on me, boys," he told them, clapping Patty on the shoulder. "After that, you're on your own."

"Geez, you get a Captain's salary," Ramirez complained. "How about buying a poor Technician First-Class dinner?"

"Only if you put out, Mule."

None of the "establishments" in the Fry had signs. You knew where you were going if you lived there, and why the hell would you be there at all if you didn't? He led them past the dance floors blasting old electronica, past the sit-down restaurants charging the better part of an average worker's weekly salary for actual cow meat imported from down south, and past one of the few occupied buildings, a brothel whose customers risked potentially unsafe buildings to have most certainly unsafe sex.

The tent he took them into wasn't quite as crowded as the others, but he preferred the atmosphere. A live band played on a stage made from storage crates, acoustic instruments belting out tunes that had been old when the Prime was a boy. There was a bar where you could order drinks and food and both weren't cheap but weren't outrageous either. Tables were whatever could be cobbled together from leavings, ranging from actual outdoor tables salvaged from pre-war restaurants to wooden spools that had once held electrical cable for utility companies, and the chairs were equally eclectic.

The clientele here was a step up from the rest of the Fry's denizens. Fewer "edgy" types with body mods and dyed skin and more normal worker types just trying to make a life in the ruins of the city, or coming in from the suburb enclaves to have a little fun. They'd dressed to fit in, since wearing flight suits out here in the World would have been an invitation to any crackpot conspiracy theorist or desperate junkie who wanted to take a shot at them and try to claim a reward from the Russians.

Nate fell into a folding bag chair with the logo of the Washington DC baseball team from a time when either of those had existed and the others sat with him for a moment, gathered around what had once been the dining room table of some nearby family. Nate sat and listened to a credible performance of "Proud Mary" by a pudgy, bald man with a curly beard down to his chest while a couple who looked to be in their sixties danced in an area clearly not designed for it, their denim vests sorting matching logos from an outlaw motorcycle gang.

"You do take a girl to the nicest places," Roach leaned over to enunciate in his ear over the music.

"We gonna get those drinks?" Ramirez whined, wincing in appreciation of the music.

Nate rolled his eyes at the kid and pulled a handful of silver coins out of his pocket, handing them over to the team Mule.

"Get me whatever beer they have on tap," he told Ramirez. "I'm feeling adventurous."

"I'll have a shot of whiskey," Roach ordered. "Make it two," she decided just as he was getting up.

"Make it four," Patty added. He still seemed morose, Nate thought. Maybe the night on the town would loosen him up.

"I gotta carry this shit all by myself?" Ramirez looked at them, scowling.

"You already know the answer to that, Mule," Roach said, waving him toward the bar.

The kid was still muttering as he left and Nate laughed softly. If they did find a replacement for Patty, at least Ramirez wouldn't be the Mule anymore.

"Hey Boss," Patty said, interrupting the thought and the music. He leaned forward over the polished oak table, jaws working at the chewing tobacco crammed into his cheek. "I just wanted to say, I know Dix was your friend, and I'm sorry about what happened. I did respect him. He was a hell of a mechanic."

"He was that," Nate agreed, wishing he already had a drink in his hand. "He learned the hard way, in a combat unit where you had to repair your own shit, just like ours. It's how Ramirez is going to have to learn, if he has the natural skills for it." He sighed out a breath, letting the table take the weight of his elbows. "And he was a guy you could count on having your back, which is even harder to find than a mechanic." He nodded to Patty. "By the way, I wanted to tell you, you kicked ass against those Tagans. You probably saved my life and Roach's getting fire on the first one so quick."

"Being fairly fucking sure you're going to die tends to focus a man," Patty said, shrugging the praise off as if he weren't comfortable with it. "Desperation makes you fast." He spat a stream of tobacco juice into a cup he'd brought along for the purpose. "Anyway, I just wanted to tell you again I was sorry I missed the funeral."

"Funeral's for the living," Nate told him, shaking his head. "We all have to deal with death in our own way."

Roach didn't say anything, but Nate noticed her poorly-hidden scowl and gathered she didn't agree. For once, though, she kept her mouth shut for the sake of team harmony and he smiled encouragingly to her. She rolled her eyes, but still remained silent until Ramirez returned with the drinks. He'd borrowed a serving tray and made a show of wiping down the table with a cloth while holding it above him one-handed.

"You spill my drink showing off," Nate warned him, only half-kidding, "you're going to be buying the replacement with your own money."

"Jeez, hard crowd," Ramirez said, but lowered the tray and handed Nate a plastic cup full of something that might have been beer and was definitely brewed locally and recently.

Nate sipped at it tentatively, then shrugged. It wasn't the worst he'd ever had, which was about all he could expect under the circumstance. The band had switched to another song by then, something he assumed was called "Come As You Are," though he couldn't quite remember the name of the group that had originally played it.

"Who sang this anyway?" he wondered aloud. Patty and Ramirez pretended not to hear him, but Roach slammed down one of her shots, then shrugged.

"Quien sabe?" she said. "All way before my time."

"Oh, never mind." He took another sip. Dix would have known the answer. He had loved old music.

Patty tipped back his second shot, slamming the glass down to the stained wood table and gasping out a breath. His eyes had rolled back slightly at the bite of the drink and when they came back level, he leaned forward, seeing something behind them. Nate glanced around but only saw a few people walking past just outside the mosquito netting.

"I'll be right back," Patty told them, rising up from the table. "I think I saw someone I know."

"How the hell does he know anyone here at all?" Roach asked, her second shot clasped between thumb and forefinger. She looked down at the amber liquid, sniffed it and made a face. "This stuff is shit," she added before drinking it anyway.

"Maybe he comes here on his off time," Ramirez ventured, shrugging indifferently and nursing his beer. Nate tried to remember if he was old enough to drink it.

"When have we had any fucking off time?" Roach shot back, glaring at the younger man.

Nate stopped paying attention to their back-and-forth when the next song began to play. It was one of his favorites, one Dix had introduced him to. It was an older song, by a group called REM. He remembered the name because of the sleep studies he'd researched trying to figure out how to beat insomnia. Rapid Eye Movement. The song was called Nightswimming and he wasn't sure why, but it always touched a nostalgia for a youth he hadn't had the chance to experience.

"Hey," he said, nodding to Roach. "Want to dance?"

Her eyebrows shot up in disbelief.

"To this old-ass shit?"

"Humor an old man." He stood and offered her a hand.

Roach sighed and rolled her eyes but took the hand and walked with him out to the open area in front of the makeshift stage. The Outlaw Biker couple was still dancing, their pace and step more sedate than it had been for the faster songs, and Roach and Nate fell into step in a rotation opposite theirs, two sets of celestial bodies in orbit around the same center of gravity.

"You sure you want to lead?" Roach asked quietly, smirking as he spun her awkwardly.

"I ask myself that question all the time," he admitted, eyes downward, watching his feet.

"We got some real problems here," Roach said, apparently intuiting that he hadn't just been speaking of dancing.

The band had a violinist, or possibly a fiddler depending on which sort of music they were playing at the time, and she hit the two-note section between verses that always hit him right in the gut. He didn't even know enough about music to put the right name to it, but whatever genius of a previous generation had written it had known how to get to someone with just a twin strum of a violin. He dipped despite the twinges in his knees and shoulder and elbow, bringing her back up smoothly. She was solid muscle and probably a good sixty kilos.

Why, he wondered inanely, *am I not attracted to her?* She's pretty, funny, spirited, intelligent... Not that he'd do anything about it—they had enough problems without the commander getting involved with one of his subordinates—but it bothered him he never even felt the stirring. Was that something else the cellular degradation was stealing from him?

"If you mean my dancing, I agree," he said. "If you mean with the team, I still agree. Unfortunately, neither is likely to improve in the immediate future."

"Maybe we need to withdraw from the area," she suggested. "We could tell DoD we needed the time to regroup after losing Dix. That's gotta be some sort of good reason for us to break contact."

"We do that," he told her, sobering, "we lose out on our current contract. They don't pay us for *any* of this deployment unless we finish the term."

"Shit," she murmured, eyes clouding over at the thought. "I need that money."

"I think we all do. Especially Patty."

The song ended and Nate clapped in appreciation while Roach looked around, eyes narrowing.

"Where the hell did he go, anyway?" she wondered.

Nate followed her gaze, couldn't find a sign of the Kentuckian anywhere.

"We'd better go see if we can find him." He fished another silver coin out of his pocket and tossed it to Ramirez on the way toward the door. "Mule, get me another beer and order me a burger, will you? And get yourself another drink. We'll be right back."

The night breeze had picked up outside and he felt it carry away the thin sheen of sweat the stuffiness under the tent had built up on his brow. Patrons and workers wandered around outside, some leaning against crumbling facades to catch a smoke, others tucked into the shadows of alleyways locked in heated embraces. Some of those would be prostitutes, freelancers who didn't work for the brothel. They were pretty rough-looking, gnawed at and eaten away by drugs and disease, and a man would have to be pretty desperate to choose that option.

Norfolk is the right place to find desperate people, though.

He and Roach wandered down the plaza from the bar, checking alleyways and shadowed corners, until they'd circled back around almost to the entrance.

"There he is," Roach said, touching his arm.

She didn't point, knowing better than to draw attention to themselves. He followed her eyes instead to the near distance, under the edge of a canopy set up for food vendors. Patty was there, hands tucked inside his pockets, shoulders hunched as if waiting for the rain to fall. Facing him was a woman who almost certainly did not belong in the Fry. She was tall, probably as tall as Nate even without the high-heeled calf boots, and slender and did wonderful things to the jeans and turtleneck she tried to pass off as casual wear, and Nate suddenly discovered that yes, he was still interested in sex.

"Jesus," Roach breathed. "She's so far out of his league, they're not even on the same planet."

"What the hell is she doing here?" he wondered. It was a better question. People with the sort of money to look that good didn't come to Norfolk, and they certainly didn't come to the Fry.

Suddenly, Patty became animated, pointing at his own chest, at her, waving expansively. Nate couldn't be sure but he thought the man was yelling, or at least speaking loudly. He didn't seem happy, which Nate couldn't imagine, not when talking to someone who was probably the most beautiful woman the Kentuckian had ever met, or would meet.

"What's going on?" Roach asked plaintively, clearly frustrated she couldn't hear them.

"Why don't you go ask them?" he suggested, only half serious.

She sniffed. "Maybe I will."

Before either of them could make a move, Patty threw his

hands up as if in exasperation and stalked away from the blond, heading deeper into the Fry around the opposite side of the plaza.

"He's pissed off," Roach observed.

"He's always pissed off." Nate shrugged. "It's her I'm curious about. Think I should go talk to her?"

"You?" Roach eyed him with a brow arched dubiously. "Maybe I should be the one to try it."

"Be my guest, Sergeant Mata," he said, waving a hand invitingly.

She headed off across the plaza, striding purposefully like a missile homing in on the blond, but she hadn't gotten more than a dozen meters or so before the mysterious woman's head snapped up and her eyes narrowed.

She's blown, Nate thought.

Sure enough, the blond disappeared into the shadows a moment later.

"Well now what?" Roach asked, coming back to him, fists clenched as if she wanted to punch someone.

"Now we go eat our burgers," he suggested. "If Patty wants to tell us what's going on, he'll have his chance."

"You're too damned patient," Roach told him as they headed back to the bar. "I hope I never get that old."

INTERLUDE:_

The cot creaked under my weight, wobbling slightly off-balance as I rolled in it, one of the rubber boots at the end of the right-hand front leg worn down further than the others. The sound and the motion only served to magnify the pain throbbing in my head, to send it bouncing back and forth from one temple to another like someone had fired a .22 round inside my skull.

How the fuck did I wind up on a cot? I forced my eyes open against the glare of far-off lights. I wasn't in my quarters. There was no closet, no wall of pictures and diplomas, no nightstand. I felt something over my legs and thought it was my flight suit just tossed on top of me. I opened my eyes completely and wiped the moisture and sleep out of them and finally saw I was in an empty room, stripped of all other furniture. It might have once been a mess hall or a briefing area, but now it was just bare walls, overhead lights...and one cot. And me.

I sat up and swung my legs off the cot, feet bare, a chill in the air that sent shivers up my back. I was wearing a T-shirt and shorts like I usually did when I slept. Everything was usual except why the hell was I in this empty room? Hell, *where* was this empty room? Hadn't I been in...was it Georgia? South Carolina?

Shit, I can't remember. They all seem to run together.

I pulled the flight suit on as if I were a puppet in someone else's hands, going through motions without any internal purpose. I found socks tucked into my combat boots and pulled them on then strapped on the boots. I looked around for anything else, for a toothbrush or soap or even a bottle of water, but there was nothing. No, wait. There was a bottle of water, tucked under the edge of the cot. I unscrewed the cap and drank it, downing it in one, long, breathless gulp, except for the last little bit. I swished that around inside my mouth before I swallowed it, trying to get rid of the dead-cat taste. It wasn't as good as brushing my teeth, but it would have to do.

I looked around for somewhere to throw the bottle away but didn't see a trash can. I shrugged and tossed it on the bunk before I headed toward the door. The double doors to the room had narrow windows set in them and through them was furtive motion, ghostlike, as if the building had been abandoned decades ago but was still haunted. I didn't believe in ghosts, so I pushed through the door.

The place was being cleared out. Everywhere I looked, cardboard boxes, plastic storage tubs, wooden crates were stacked beside doorways. Men and women in Army battle utilities were carrying armloads out towards an open doorway, like a colony of ants taking food to their queen. I moved through them, staring at each face, trying to find one I remembered. They were strangers. They didn't meet my eyes, avoided looking at me, as if I were the ghost haunting them.

I wandered out the front door into the morning light. It felt warmer out in the sun and I wondered what month it was.

How did I not know what month it was?

The trees were pine and oak crowding in around cracked

pavement and square, unimaginative buildings and I could have been anywhere. Well, anywhere they didn't have mountains because it looked pretty flat out here, not a hill or mountain to be seen over the tree line.

Cargo trucks were idling impatiently in the street in front of the building, as if they were ready to run and resented having to wait for the line of soldiers loading boxes and crates and duffle bags into their covered beds. Each was guarded by at least a couple armed soldiers, visors shut on full-head helmets I didn't remember seeing before. They carried standard M37 carbines, though. Some things never changed. I remembered how new those had used to seem when they finally replaced the old M4's.

Wait. How along ago was that? How can I remember that?

"Captain Stout?"

I turned at the call and saw an incredibly young second lieutenant jogging up to me, out of breath, holding her hat on against the breeze, her blond hair matted with sweat.

"That's me."

"Sir," she said, seeming slightly uncomfortable calling me that, her eyes not quite willing to meet mine, "Colonel Solana wants to see you in his office."

"He still has an office?" I chuckled, but her face remained totally serious, as if I hadn't spoken at all. "Okay, Lieutenant, lead on."

We walked with purposeful quickness, circumnavigating the building where I'd woken and heading for another, smaller, connected to the first with a covered walkway. No one stopped to salute either of us, even the ones who didn't have their hands full. I thought that was curious, but I said nothing.

"What's the hurry?" I asked her. "Why's everyone pulling out?"

"The Colonel will give you all the information you need, sir."

Well, that *was rude.*

I thought about pulling rank on her, but I'm a pilot and we aren't too good at that. For pilots, rank is more about how few people can actually tell you what to do instead of how many people you can order around. So I just waited patiently and squeezed past at least a dozen more enlisted grunts pushing handcarts or operating motorized pallet jacks through the hallways of the smaller building.

Colonel Solana's office was still furnished, though it, too, was stuffed with packed boxes, the shelves and desk bare of any accoutrements or personal items. Solana himself was short and grey-haired and looked like a man who'd just come home from a three-day bender, with bags under his puffy eyes and deep lines in his face. He'd been typing a report into a tablet when we arrived at his open door and barely looked up at our presence. The lieutenant saluted him and announced our arrival, but Solana just waved her away.

"Sit down, Stout," he said, nodding toward the folding chair in front of his cheap, pressed-wood desk.

Solana's hands seemed to want to go back to typing and he visibly pulled them away from the keyboard and made himself face me.

"Okay, we don't have a lot of time. The Army is pulling out of here..."

"Sorry, sir," I interrupted, "but where is *here*?"

He sighed, rubbing a hand over his eyes.

"Shit, you still don't remember everything yet, do you? Why the hell did those stupid DoD fuckers drop you off when they fucking *knew* we didn't have a use for you?"

I didn't have an answer for that, didn't even understand the question, so I didn't say anything. Solana raised his hands palms out as if he were about to launch into a lecture.

"Okay, I'll make this quick, because we don't have time for

anything else. You're a dupe, Stout. A genetic duplicate of the original Nathan Stout, who lived like thirty fucking years ago. He volunteered for the dupe program because the guy who came up with the mechs was his friend, Robert Franklin and he knew there was no other way the DoD would approve them with the radiation leakage from the isotope reactors."

You ever splashed ice-cold water in your face on a chilly morning, just to wake up, knowing how painful it's going to be? That was me, right then. Everything he said was true, and I remembered it as he said it as if a veil had been lifted off my eyes.

"But the program's over now," he went on, finally telling me something I *didn't* know. "We just got our first batch of the new Hellfire mechs with the new radiation shielding. They finally cracked the problem and anyone can pilot a mech without risking dying of cancer in twenty years. You were the last of the bunch cloned before they shut it down and the stupid assholes at DoD shipped you out here like clockwork anyway after the last version of you bought it on a mission. But we're pulling out of Maryland and there are already enough pilots where we're heading, so we don't need you." He shrugged. "You got a choice here. You can either go with us and spend the rest of your life being a gopher stuck running whatever errands the Army can find for you, or you can take your discharge, along with a hell of a lot of back pay from your various incarnations, and stay here."

"You're pulling out of here," I said numbly. "The Russians are still pushing in, trying to take the eastern seaboard. What the hell would I do here?"

"There's a new program the DoD is marching out," Solana told me. He seemed genuinely interested now, and I had the sense that if he were a younger man, he would have done it himself, although that might have been salesmanship. "It's called Broken Arrow, and basically, you'd be a private military contractor working for them. You'd recruit your own team through a list of candidates who'll receive free DoD training on piloting and maintaining and repairing Hellfires, and the government would supply you with weapons and ammo and spare parts and send you on assignments where needed."

I shook my head, confused.

"How is that any different from just keeping the Army out here?" I wondered.

"Because the government ain't paying for medical treatment, insurance, retirement, housing, transportation, food, support..." He shrugged. "Need I go on? It's a million times cheaper to pay you a contract fee, give you the weapons you need and let you take care of the rest." He grinned, again with that sense of almost envy. "And you'll be in charge. No one looking over your shoulder, no one telling you to police your mustache, tuck in your shirt, paint the fucking rocks in the parking lot."

I nodded slowly. It was a lot to take in, but...

"You know, that doesn't sound too bad."

And it wasn't as if I had a long life or a retirement ahead of me anyway. The family I remembered, what little I remembered of them, was long gone, probably dead, certainly very old. And these people obviously thought of me as a freak, and not even a useful one anymore. Travelling with them out west so they could stick me cleaning toilets didn't sound at all appealing.

"Where do I sign up?" I asked him, the decision making itself for me.

"Not here," Solana said, gesturing around us at the disarray. "I'll get you a flight out to the DoD liaison office in Philadelphia. They're handling the Broken Arrow program from there." He stood and so did I, not forgetting that bit of military courtesy despite all the other things the original Nate Stout had known and not passed down to me. "Good luck, Stout. Take the fight to those Russian bastards. Maybe you can finish what we started."

He offered a hand and I shook it. He was still being a salesman, closing the deal. I wondered exactly what I was buying into.

CHAPTER TEN_

That bitch. Patty took a long swig of the moonshine, feeling the tiny, jagged cracks in the mouth of the used and used and reused bottle he'd had to pay a premium to take out of the bar. The home brew steamrolled down his throat and crashed with fiery finality in his stomach, numbing mercifully behind it, making it easier for the next hit.

"That fucking bitch." He said it aloud because there was no one around to hear it. He looked down at the remains of the Tagan U-mech. They'd hauled with them from the warehouse and it made a convenient seat, resting on a pallet on the tiled floor.

He'd come back to the base, paying for a ride in a pedicab until he was close enough to walk because he hadn't wanted to ride back in the truck with the others. He couldn't look them in the face right now. He couldn't believe Svetlana had taken the risk of showing up at the Fry. Was she monitoring him? Had she concealed a bug somewhere in his clothes when they were together? Did she know he'd been thinking of leaving? Why else would she be there?

She'd denied it of course. Her words played in his mind over and over, like those After-Action Reviews Dix had always insisted they have after every mission.

"I am here because our sources said you were headed here," she'd told him, calm and unflappable in the face of his consternation. "I was concerned there might be a problem so I came to see if you required assistance."

"And what if they saw you?" he raged, waving his arms back toward the bar where the others were. "What if they see us together?"

She snorted a laugh. "Then they'll believe you are, as they say, punching outside your weight."

"You think this is fucking funny?" he demanded. "You told me you weren't going to kill any of them! You promised me!"

"I promised I would *try* not to kill them," she corrected him. "If it were possible. But I am not always the one with the final say. You forget, Geoffrey, I too work for someone and they make the choice whether or not to listen to my recommendations."

"And their choice was to take me off the table?" He thumped a finger into his chest. "Am I not useful to your boss anymore? He thinks he can just toss me out with the trash and save himself the money?"

"It was a golden opportunity. Everyone was gathered together, outside their mechs. We thought we could take what we needed and be out before there was any fighting. We did not anticipate the defense system." She shot him a glare. "You did not *inform* us of the defense system."

"Because they don't tell me shit like that!" he insisted. "That's the sort of shit Dix and Nate handled! I'm not a tech or a mechanic, just a pilot!"

"If you want to be important enough to my boss to *not* be disposable," she said, cocking her head toward him, "it's something you need to find out and pass on. Otherwise, why would he bother to keep you around, as you say? Why not just save himself the money and the trouble?"

He took a deep breath and tried to control himself. Yelling at her would only draw more attention.

"I will be in touch, Geoffrey. Until then, I suggest you learn as much as you can and endeavor to make yourself useful."

With that, he'd left her there and gone off to get drunk. Alone.

"I'm better off alone," he murmured at the mechs surrounding him, standing in silent judgement.

"You always talk to yourself when you're drunk?"

Roach's voice scared the shit out of him and he jumped up from the chest panel of the ruined Tagan, holding his bottle back defensively, as if someone was about to try to grab it from him.

"How the fuck do you move so quiet?" he asked, finally spotting her coming in the doorway from the outer hall.

"Everyone's quiet when your head's buzzing that loud, man," Ramirez said with a wry grin, coming out behind her.

Nate was last. He didn't look mad, just disappointed. He always seemed disappointed when he looked at Patty. Just like his mom.

"Where'd you get off to, Patty?" Nate asked him, tone soft and even. "We were worried about you."

"I'm still here, man," he muttered, not meeting the man's eyes. He took another hit from the bottle. "Isn't that all that's important? That I stay here and pilot a mech for God and fucking country?"

"Come on, Nate," Roach urged him, motioning past him to the entrance to the offices where they'd made their quarters. "You aren't going to get anything coherent out of him right now. Everything right now's the alcohol talking."

"In wine is truth," Nate said, eyes locked on Patty, boring into him. "I wonder what's in moonshine?"

"Bullshit, I'd guess," Roach told him. She pushed him toward the door.

Patty wanted to ask Nate if he was getting any of that, but he wasn't *quite* drunk enough for that. Roach was dangerous. He chuckled at the thought, then laughed outright as the two of them disappeared through the interior doorway.

"What's so damn funny, Patty?" Ramirez asked him. He wasn't leaving, was just standing there, hands on his hips, watching Patty like he expected him to start doing tricks. "You think it's so fucking hilarious you're alienating everyone? Dude, there's only four of us now! We need to stick together and you keep pushing everyone away."

Patty shook his head. The Mule didn't know. He couldn't know. *I should tell him.*

He took another drink, a long one. Everything was numb now, from head to toe, and the moonshine felt smoother going down.

"Dix is dead because of me." He'd blurted it out, but not the confession he'd meant. The words wouldn't come.

"That ain't true, man," Ramirez insisted, rubbing a hand over his neck as if the words made him feel uncomfortable. "There was nothing you could have done."

He laughed. He hadn't meant to, but the laughter bubbled out of him, harsh and bitter, almost a sob.

"If y'all knew what I'd done in my life," he said, "you'd all hate me. You wouldn't want to stand here talking to me."

"What we did before doesn't matter. I was in some trouble when I was a kid." Ramirez shrugged. "Did some bad things, but when the Department of Defense came and offered me the chance to take mech pilot training and get my record wiped, I figured it was my chance for a new start. You can make a new life if you don't like your old one."

"However many lives I lead, Mule," he said, the laughter sputtering out, dying to a trickle, "I'll fuck them all up in the end. It's what I do, man. It's who I am."

"I don't know what you mean, Patty. What have you done that's so much worse than the rest of us?"

"Nothing." He looked down at the bottle. It was only about half empty, but he couldn't force himself to drink any more of it. The answers weren't in there. "Nothing worth talking about.

He whipped the bottle underhanded at the Tagan, lashing out at everything it represented. It shattered, ancient glass older than him, older than his grandmother. Destroyed now, just like everything else in the world that had created it. Ramirez flinched at the explosion of glass and the sudden, powerful stench of grain alcohol.

"You should get away from here, Mule," he warned the man. "Get out of here before we all wind up dead."

Svetlana Grigoryeva hated the city. It wasn't the destruction or the dirt or the crime that bothered her. No, those reminded her of home, of how Ekaterinburg had been since she was a little girl. She'd seen old videos and pictures of it before the war, before the drone strikes had levelled it, when the old churches had still stood, and the old auditorium had still been in use. Now all of it was laid waste and humans lived in the wreckage and fought for scraps beside the dogs and the rats.

No, she hated Norfolk because the people here still believed, still had hope. They still hung American flags outside their front doors and raked the yards of their crumbling houses and thought that someday, if they just held out long enough, the

American government would come back and save them. In Russia, everyone *knew* the government would never help, whether it was strong or weak. The government was a parasite living off the failing body of a dying man. She would have thought Americans would understand that by now but still they deceived themselves.

It was better at night. Night was when the true believers retreated back behind their barred doors and padlocks, counting on their shotguns and prayer to get them to the morning. The only people on the street at night knew the truth, knew their place in this new world.

She spotted them immediately, blocks away, but she kept walking straight ahead because to show weakness would have been worse. Better to confront a predator than to have them stalk you, unseen. They were gathered around a trio of fifty-five-gallon drums, flames licking out over the openings, smoke drifting off to the north, gathering in the gaps between buildings as if afraid to rise above the rooftops and show itself to the greater world.

It was her first indication. There was no need for a fire tonight. If it was cool, it was only by comparison with the brutal humidity of mid-day. The fires were bait, to draw in victims. Three ancient supermarket baskets packed with all the belongings of a life spent on the street rested half in the shadows a few meters outside the overlapping circles of light, but none belonged to any of these three men. They didn't live on these streets, they were far too clean for that, their clothes roughly made but well kept, camouflage.

She kept her hands in her jacket pockets and kept walking. Her path would take her exactly four meters to the right of the right-most trash barrel, four meters from the partially collapsed front wall of what used to be a clothing store. She could move further over with a few steps to the right, but she'd be taking the chance they didn't have a fourth man concealed in the store. And it would be a man. These weren't progressive, equal opportunity bangers, they had an agenda...or possibly a menu. And she was on it.

The soles of her boots clopped hollow on the pavement, even, steady steps. The three men watched her with predator's eyes and said not a word. No banter, no catcalls, no invitations to come "party" with them. They hadn't the need to try to work themselves up for this, to escalate the interaction and justify their actions by some pretense she had disrespected them or led them on. Men of that sort were easier to deal with, easier to cow with a few words and a hard glare. Words wouldn't be an option here.

The fingers of her right hand curled tightly around the cold, metal grip of the compact pistol in her jacket pocket. She wondered if she'd have to kill all of them or if shooting the first one would scare off the others.

They waited until she was almost past them, till her eyes flickered to her left to keep them in her line of sight. They'd been silent, almost motionless, as if they thought they could blend into the background. The moment her head turned just an almost-imperceptible fraction of an inch, the one closest to her lunged for her. It was a practiced move, the crack of a whip, his hand aimed toward her elbow. Smart, not going for the wrist. The wrist could be pulled away more quickly. The elbow required a full body move.

She was prepared. She took a half-step back with her left foot, a natural motion, squaring her up against the man as he went off-balance from the missed grab, all of his weight on his plant leg, the one closest to her. Her left foot snapped out, a striking cobra, catching him in the kneecap. The sound was a maul hitting a fencepost, the feeling a seashell cracking under an errant step. He screamed, dreadlocks flashing in the glow of the trash fires, teeth white and even until the butt of her pistol cracked into his face and broke three of them off at the gumline. Blood sprayed and his scream became muffled as his hands went to his mouth.

He was falling, but she didn't let him. Her left arm snaked around his neck, the barrel of the cheaply-fabricated Russian handgun pressing into his temple as she dragged him backwards. The other three were frozen, their eyes wide and white, mouths half-open as if about to issue a warning.

"How important is he to you?" she wondered.

She could hear the trace of her accent in her voice. Most people couldn't detect their own accents—it was a mental blind spot. Part of her training had been to do just that, to eliminate it when she needed to. There was no need at the moment, and she liked the measure of exotic strangeness it gave her.

"Is he worth dying for?" she pressed, still dragging him in long, retreating steps, almost to the curve in the road now. "Is he your brother? Your cousin?"

One more step and she stopped. The man was begging now, his words nearly incomprehensible through swollen lips and a mouthful of blood.

"Please..."

She pulled the trigger.

The gunshot was still echoing between the buildings when the man's body hit the pavement with an obscene, wet splat. She could taste his blood on the corner of her lip, but she didn't wipe it off, didn't check her jacket for splatter. She met their eyes, showing them how little his life had meant to her, how easy it would be for her to kill each and every one of them.

She turned and rounded the corner casually, as if completely unconcerned, then ducked into a shadowy corner the moment she was out of their sight, gun raised, waiting. Mumbled words clattered off the pavement, punctuated by an exclamation, a curse. They didn't come. They weren't going to risk following her. Good. Gunshots, like carrion, attracted scavengers.

She tucked the Makarov away and walked. You never ran, not unless your life depended on it. It was the same here as in the wild, those who ran looked like prey. The crumbling ruins began to give way to buildings better kept and recently repaired, the businesses still running against all odds in this city. The resilience of the human animal sometimes astounded her. There were lights here, not battery powered lanterns but real street lights, signs, as if it were any other day before the world had fallen in on itself.

Garry's Machine and Tool.

Trang International and Interstate Shipping Service. *I imagine one is just about as difficult as the other these days.*

Benitez Bulk Food Service. That one was fortified with metal roll-up doors and barred windows. Food was more valuable than gold many places, and people would kill for it in quantity. She'd have been willing to bet this Benitez had armed guards during the day, and there might have even been a sniper or two on the roof covering the street during the night.

The businesses doubled as homes in most cases, because even the comparatively wealthy couldn't afford to maintain security on a house and a business both. One or two showed a light in an upper window. The power was on here, for those who could afford it. The plant had been built privately because there was no government to pay for it, and if there had been, it would never have passed emissions standards. It burned sewage, trash, alcohol, methane, whatever one cared to throw into it, and did it quite efficiently, particularly since they weren't at all worried about polluting the air.

It hardly seemed to matter when the filthy water and background radiation would likely give them cancer long before the dirty air. She could understand the sentiment; it was almost Russian in its pragmatism.

There were cars here as well, most of them electric, recharged from the same high-priced power, though the larger cargo trucks would probably be fueled by alcohol distilled locally. She imagined they were for local travel only, since trying to circumnavigate the downed bridges and blocked highways would have been suicide.

At the edge of the business district, she found the building she sought. It had no sign, no number, no metal doors, nothing at all to distinguish it. You simply had to know where it was. She ignored the front entrance, knowing it was blocked from inside and unusable, instead walking into the deep shadows of the alleyway between it and the next building over, abandoned and shuttered. The side door was concealed in darkness, but a knock against it revealed a solid metal core.

There was no answer, no one demanding who was there. They'd be watching her via an infrared camera, probably had been during her approach on the main road. She waited, knowing they were likely checking back along her route, making sure she hadn't been followed. Still, the loud clank of the lock when it was thrown startled her and she fought not to jump. They'd see it on the monitors and it would make them think less of her, chip away at the mystique she'd built. It was important to be feared by your enemies, but nearly as vital to be respected by your allies.

The door swung inward on well-oiled hinges and she slipped into the darkness. She heard it slam shut behind her and waited, eyes slitted, knowing the light was coming. When it did, it was harsh and naked and glaring, turning the man who'd opened the door into a blurry silhouette until her vision adjusted. He looked better as a blur, she decided. His beard was patchy, trying unsuccessfully to hide the damage of childhood acne, and his nose was a testament to punches not adequately ducked. He tried to make up for his looks with impeccable clothing, but the silk suits seemed out of place. He was a man who belonged in rough clothes to match his demeanor.

"Good evening, Ms. Grigoryeva," he said in an attempt at pleasantries. His voice was as harsh and gravelly as his face, but she smiled thinly in return. The man did his job, which was much more important than his appearance.

"Good morning, Alexie," she corrected him. "I hope I am not keeping you awake."

"I have always been nocturnal," he said, waving it off. "If I were more handsome, I might be able to pass myself off as a vampire."

"Just as well you're not." She sniffed a quiet laugh. "There are too many seeking to drain the blood of this place."

He frowned, looking more closely at her jacket. She realized she still had drops of blood painting abstract patterns across her sleeve and left lapel and she dabbed at it with a studied lack of concern.

"Did you have any problems getting here?" he wondered.

"Nothing worth speaking of," she said. Just another block added to the wall of her reputation. Every little bit helped. "He is waiting for me," she added, to shut down further conversation.

Alexie nodded and waved for her to follow.

The stairwell was dimly light, a prelude for what waited below in the basement. *He* didn't like bright lights. She guessed they bothered his eyes, though she'd never considered it worth the risk to ask him. He'd always given her the impression information was a precious commodity, handed out sparingly, and she didn't want to waste her limit on inanities. More of his men were stretched out on couches and cots in what had once been a storage room, some of them still in business suits with ties and dress shoes, others stripped down to underwear but all with a weapon close to hand. Two of the men were snoring violently, an assault on the senses that would have forced her to knife at least one of them in their sleep, but it didn't seem to keep any of the others up.

Alexie led her through the obstacle course of sleeping Russian muscle, past a wall of racked automatic weapons and at least two missile launchers to a door. It had once been a private office for a very successful businessman and she supposed, in a way, it still was. The door was soundproofed and sturdy, whether for privacy during business meetings or to keep his affairs secret from his wife, she couldn't say. It amused her to imagine the lives of those who'd lived in Norfolk before it had died, their aspirations and failings, their dalliances and daydreams. They'd probably believed it would go on forever...

Alexie didn't knock. *He* didn't like knocking either. Instead, Alexie pushed a button on what had been a receptionist's desk and the intercom buzzed for attention.

"Yes?" The voice was raspy, damaged, telling nothing about the man who'd used it when he'd been whole.

"She's here," Alexie reported, simply, efficiently.

There was no reply but a soft click of a lock releasing and the door swung inward a few centimeters. She favored Alexie with a thin smile and edged through the doorway, not opening it any further than she had to and pushing it shut behind her immediately.

The office was large and well-appointed, the furniture luxurious and pre-war in its style, polished mahogany. A single lamp burned over the desk, a reading light barely bright enough to reach the edges of the room, and *he* stood in the darkness of a corner, hands clasped behind his back as he examined the contents of a narrow bookcase. It had probably been more for decoration than education, but you could still learn much of a man or woman by what they considered intellectually impressive.

Over his shoulder, past a mane of greying hair, she could read some of the titles.

1984. The Catcher in the Rye. Pride and Prejudice. Crime and Punishment. The Art of War.

More. History books, popularized science, philosophy, self-help. Books the man who'd owned this place had thought he should have read, or thought other people would believe he should have read. Telling her nothing about that long-dead man himself except, perhaps, that he had either eclectic taste in literature or no taste of his own at all and it was a pretense. Then she spotted something more informative, something that didn't fit with the rest, and she smiled, chuckled softly.

"You saw it," he said, and she knew he'd heard her quiet laugh. "You saw the book."

Daring, she reached past his shoulder and pulled it out. The pages were brittle with age, but you could tell it had been well-read, corners folded over to mark a place.

"Teenage girls and sparkly vampires," she murmured, pushing it back into its space on the shelf. "The one thing here he'd actually read."

"You asked to see me." He turned, not toward her but into the darkness of the other side of the room, stepping away, walking stiffly like an old man plagued by arthritis. He fell onto the rich leather of a small sofa, sighing with the relief of sitting. "I have to believe you did not come to share good news."

"It's our man Patterson." She tried not to sound apologetic. She had done nothing wrong. God had made the big, dumb, Kentucky hick the way he was and she was simply stuck with him. "He's less stable than I'd hoped. I am becoming concerned he is no longer reliable. I believe he may be about to run, to try to head back to his home." She sniffed. "How he expects to make it there with no support, God alone knows."

"Do you believe in God, Svetlana?"

She blinked at the question. He'd never been so personal before.

"My parents did," she answered. "I have never given it much consideration. If He indeed exists, we must be such a disappointment."

"I did once." Very unlike him, this meandering. Was he ill? He leaned back in the couch, his head resting on the cushion, dark eyes nearly lost in the shadows. "I believed God was the Great Engineer, and the universe his grand machine, designed to wind down in just the way He'd intended so He'd never have to adjust or maintain or repair it, everything moving in a dance He'd seen at the beginning. Then I learned how truly chaotic and meaningless this universe is, how we each shape it with our misdeeds, the pebbles we carelessly toss into the pond." A rasping breath shuddered from his chest. "Now I've come to think that God is something we invented because it's simply too terrifying to admit we're aimless billiard balls randomly ricocheting through the cosmos." His head came up, the eyes sparkling by the reading lamp as they met hers.

"Do what you must to ensure he stays until we no longer need him. I'm certain if there is a God, He'll understand."

CHAPTER ELEVEN_

"I ain't getting shit out of this, boss," Ramirez admitted, waving a hand at the screen of the tablet propped up against the Tagan's CPU on the tabletop. The table was solid metal and Nate thought it had once been used for food preparation but they'd found it knocked on its side and pushed up against one of the exterior doors. "It got knocked around too much during the attack. Maybe a computer forensics lab could put it back together." He looked up, his baby face seeming even younger for a moment. "Maybe you could get the DoD support guys on it?"

Nate sighed and rubbed at his eyes, propping his feet up on the slats of the stool and resting his elbows on his knees. He was exhausted. The nightmares wouldn't stop. No matter how much he drank or how many pills he popped before bed, he woke up screaming, tasting Bryan Richardson's blood, feeling the sticky wetness plastered against his chest and face, the sickly-sweet smell of it choking him.

"I can try," he said, careful not to get Ramirez's hopes up too much. "But if they had those kinds of resources out here, they wouldn't need contractors like us. What about the other Tagans, the ones we took out at the warehouse? You get anything from them before we evacuated?"

"I could only grab the CPU out of one of them." Ramirez made a face like he was about to throw up. "And the fucking pilot was splattered all over it. But it's pretty fried too, and it's mostly just operational stuff since it was a Pi-Mech without the sort of remote piloting hardware a U-mech would have."

"All right, I'll make the call," Nate told him, standing up from the stool and leaving Ramirez to his task.

The old conference room where they'd set up the table had ample windows, most of them broken, but it provided plenty of light without having to set up the lanterns. They only had so many of those and so many batteries to go around. Nate limped out into the hallway, dim and shadowy even at mid-morning. The walls were stained and peeling and there wasn't much they could do about it, though they'd swept the floor and mopped it with bleach.

"This place isn't exactly the Ritz-Carlton," he muttered to himself as he stepped into the former garage where they'd stored the mechs.

"What's a Ritz-Carlton?" Roach asked him. He nearly jumped; he hadn't seen her there, nestled in beside her Hellfire on a stepladder, working at one of the hip-joints.

She looked as tired as he was, with the added effect of grease and dirt smeared on her face and hands.

"Someplace I was never rich enough to stay," he clarified. In actuality, he'd never been alive to see one, but his Prime had known what it was. "I'm going to send a message to the DoD Liaison Office and see if we can get some support on this."

"Yeah, good luck with that." She snorted a skeptical laugh. "When was the last time they gave us anything but ammo and spare parts?"

"I know," he admitted, shrugging helplessly. "But Ramirez doesn't have the equipment or the skill to coax anything more out of the CPUs we retrieved and we're not doing much more than sitting around licking our wounds here."

"*Buena suerte,*" she said, wishing him good luck. He understood the Spanish. The Prime had taken it in college, then gone to a Defense Language Institute course before he'd been stationed in Venezuela.

I wonder if Venezuela even exists anymore? The last he'd heard, Brazil had invaded in their quest to unite most of South America under one government. *The one government that doesn't speak fucking Spanish. Ironic.*

But that had been... His head spun for a moment as he tried to remember if he'd heard the news himself or it had been something passed on from his Prime. It had been seven years ago, the last time he'd read any news on South America. He felt dizzy and reached out a hand to steady himself against the leg of Roach's Hellfire.

"You all right, Nate?" she asked him, coming down the stepladder and putting a supportive hand on his arm. "You look like you're about to pass out."

"Not getting much sleep," he admitted. Normally, he wouldn't have even said that much, but he was starting to wonder what the point was of being stoic when everything was falling apart. "Another reason I need to ask for some support. We need more crew here, Rachel."

"We need competent people," she corrected him, arching an eyebrow. "All DoD is going to send us is more guys like Patty. He's enough problems by himself."

"Where is he?" Nate glanced around, hoping the man wasn't standing right there listening to them talk about him. "I haven't seen him since last night."

"Who the hell knows?" She tossed down the wrench she

still held, letting it clatter back into the open tool box beside the ladder. "Still sleeping it off maybe. He can fucking stay out of my way for the next few hours unless he wants a kick in the ass."

"Maybe I should just let him go," Nate mused. "He's no use to us if he's sitting around feeling sorry for himself."

"He leaves here on his own," Roach said, "and he's never going to make it back to Kentucky. His only chance is a MAC flight and they don't give those spots to civilians who didn't live up to their contract."

He nodded. Military Airlift Command would let contractors who were finished with their commitment fly Space-A in cargo birds back to the closest air base to their home, but Patty wouldn't have that option if he took off now. He'd have to try to buy his way on a boat or an overland cargo convoy, maybe hire on as security. The odds weren't great.

The satellite communication gear was set up near the largest of the broken windows, the only one in the garage they hadn't boarded up the first day. The dish was fixed to the window sill with a C-clamp, the cables running back down to a folding table they'd found in a closet. The actual sat-com was small, about the size of a cell phone, but it was hooked up to a keyboard and monitor along with a 3-D scanner and printer because you didn't want to have to run to wherever the Department of Defense's nearest contractor liaison happened to have an office to get every little thing you might need.

Too bad we can't print a new mech pilot with the damned thing.

He powered on the sat com and monitor and waited way too long for it to boot up. He remembered, through the eyes of the Prime, a time when computers had booted up quicker than this. Was this just an old machine trying to run new software or was it due to the added security for a military program?

The prompt blinked on the screen and he typed in his code

word, the identifier to let someone on the other end know who was connecting. Then came the questions. Password. ID number. Date of birth. He'd made something up for that one back when he'd first signed up for the Contractor program—no one was going to believe he was seven. Same for place of birth, though for different reasons. He couldn't remember where he'd been gestated, just where he'd woken up. It was on a military base, of course.

Finally, the system gave him access and he navigated to the help screen and chose "chat with a live representative," then waited again, much longer this time.

"How much you want to bet the guy who talks with you on that thing is somewhere in Malaysia or east Africa?" Roach cracked, back to working on her mech.

He didn't comment. It was an old joke, one he'd stopped laughing at and then stopped trying to discourage her from repeating because what was the point?

THIS IS CONTRACTOR LIAISON, the chat program responded after nearly ten minutes. MY NAME IS CHAD. HOW MAY I HELP YOU TODAY, CAPTAIN STOUT?

He'd been thinking about what to say for hours now, but it still took him a long several seconds of consideration before he began typing.

HAVE LOST A MAN KIA. TWO ENEMY ATTACKS HAVE SHOWN INSIDE KNOWLEDGE OF OUR LOCATION AND TACTICS. NO SIGN OF OBJECTIVE AND NO INDICATION OF WHERE THE ENEMY IS BASED. He left out the part about Langley. Even if they believed it, there was nothing they could do about it. REQUIRE A REPLACEMENT PILOT ASAP WITH PRE-WAR MILITARY EXPERIENCE. REQUIRE GUIDANCE AS TO OBJECTIVES.

PLEASE WAIT WHILE I REFER YOUR REQUEST TO THE PROPER DEPARTMENT.

He'd seen *that* one coming. He expected it at least once more, but he'd copied the text onto his clipboard to re-use when he had to repeat it again. And again. He went through the original guy with the dubious name of Chad, to Eric in Contractor Relations, to Fiona, supposedly Eric's manger and finally, blissfully, to Charlotte who actually worked for the Department of Defense. He pasted his request again and there was no response for nearly ten minutes. He was starting to worry he'd lost the data connection, but then something totally unexpected happened. The screen flashed: **CONNECTION INTERRUPTED**, and the sat phone began ringing.

Roach stared at him and he shook his head. They'd never called before. He picked up the handset and pushed the flashing green button on the screen. He nearly just gave an inane "hello," but decided it wouldn't sound professional.

"Stout," he said instead.

"I'm looking at your official roster," a woman's voice said without preamble or introduction. Was this Charlotte? "Who did you lose?"

"Dix," he said quickly, then elaborated. "Lt. Bryan Richardson, formerly US Navy. He was our computer guy and our chief repair tech. We're having trouble maintaining the gear without him."

And maintaining our mental stability, he thought but didn't add. Didn't want to give higher a reason to revoke their contract.

"What is the situation with respect to your objective?"

He bit down on the profanity he wanted to reply with.

"We received intelligence about a possible shipping location a few days ago and when we went to check it out, it was an ambush. We fought through it without casualties, but the enemy Tagan we captured was a U-Mech remotely piloted via satellite and we couldn't get anything useful from it. While we were examining it, we were attacked by multiple Tagans at our assigned primary home base for this mission and Dix was fatally injured almost at once. We defeated the enemy but had to move to our secondary base and have received no further intelligence." He paused, and when she didn't respond, he felt compelled to continue. "Honestly, we're starting to feel like our asses are hanging in the wind here. We need another pilot with maintenance experience and we really need some guidance from higher."

He felt his stomach turn backflips. He hadn't spoken to anyone at the DoD since he'd finished his training course for contractor work and received his permit, now here he was running to them with his tail between his legs. He half expected Charlotte, or whoever was on the phone with him, to snap at him to man up and get back to work.

"Wait one, Stout."

Sure, I'll wait, he yelled at her inside his head. *Where the hell am I going to go?*

Charlotte came back two minutes later, not pissed off or annoyed as he thought she'd be. She seemed concerned, or else very skilled at faking it.

"Stout, we need you to hold in place until we can get you a new target. The enemy has gone silent but we have reason to believe they're still in the area." She hesitated, as if unused to sharing this much information with her contractors. "It's almost as if they're waiting for something, but we have no clue what. As for your personnel issues, we...might have someone we can send you. He isn't ideal, but he's the best we can do and he has the experience you need. Be aware, it may take as long as three weeks before he can get there."

"I copy that," Nate said, trying to keep the excitement out of his voice. "Will comply. Thank you."

He made sure she was done speaking before he touched the

button to disconnect the call and looked up at Roach's expectant, questioning stare.

"They're going to send us a replacement, but it might take a couple weeks." He shrugged. "She also said he wasn't ideal, whatever that means."

"Like any of us are ideal. What about the mission?"

"They're trying to get more information." Nate shrugged. "They want us to stand by and not make any moves until they can get a better handle on things."

Roach grunted thoughtfully.

"I'm not sure if I feel good that they're being honest with us or worried they really do know as little as we always thought they did."

"I'm going to hold onto the positive for the moment," Nate declared, slapping a palm on the table as he rose. "And I'm going to go tell Ramirez the good news. If you see Patty, let him know."

"I'll tell him," she promised, "right after I kick him in the ass."

Geoff Patterson wasn't hiding... not exactly. He'd just decided to explore a part of the Coast Guard base away from where he knew everyone else would be.

The place was creepy. The warehouse where they'd been was small, self-contained, a kind of a shell against the devastating loneliness of the Norfolk docks. The Coast Guard base was huge and sprawling and it seemed like every dark corner or shadowed alcove held a threat, an enemy, a monster. Patty had hoped to find some old lost treasure, something overlooked by decades' worth of looting, but the closest he'd come was when he'd stumbled on an old break room, complete with snack and soda machines. The front display panels were busted out and everything had been looted out of them decades ago. The money was still there, coins scattered across the tile floor, worthless now since the government had adjusted for the hyperinflation that had followed the outbreak of the war. No paper money, though.

Someone probably grabbed it to wipe their ass with. Or maybe to paper their wall.

He sat down in one of the uncomfortable white plastic chairs in the break room and stared up at a tattered information poster detailing the new minimum and maximum ages to enlist in the military back about thirty years ago. The minimum age, it informed him, was now sixteen, while the maximum age had been extended to fifty.

Nowadays, the military barely accepted any recruits, and put the ones who did enlist through excruciating tests to make sure they were physically and mentally fit. There just wasn't any money to pay for food and medical care and retirement and housing for dead weight. Contractors were much cheaper, and much more disposable.

His cell phone chirped at him with annoying cheerfulness and he scowled. He needed to remember to delete the ringer on the damned thing. It would be Roach or Nate bugging him again, wanting to know where he was, wanting to know why he wasn't doing his share of the work, because they and Ramirez were the only ones who could access the phone. The only cell towers that had any power going to them were the military ones and the ones paid for by people like the little enclaves in Norfolk who still had money, still tried to run their businesses. None of those would reach here.

He tried to ignore the phone, but it kept signaling, vibrating and finally he cursed and yanked it off his belt clip, half intending to throw it across the room to join the wrecked vending machines as a testament to a lost world. Then he saw the incoming call icon and the name hovering above it and his hand froze.

"No fucking way," he murmured.

It was his mother's number, in Kentucky. There was no way in hell she should be able to contact him out here. He hit the answer button with trembling fingers and put the phone to his ear.

"Mom?" he asked, his voice sounding young and hesitant. "Mom, is that you?"

"Sorry, little Geoffrey, but it's not Mommy."

His blood froze at the voice on the other end of the line. It was smooth and husky and familiar, with the bite of a shot of cheap vodka.

"Svetlana, why did you call me? How did you get my mom's number?"

Both were, he recognized immediately, very stupid questions, but they were placeholders to buy time until he could think of something more intelligent to say.

"Never mind that now, Geoffrey," she said, dismissing what he'd said as if she'd already discerned its unimportance. "For now, I think the most important thing for you to consider is the video clip I've attached to the message I've just sent you. Please go ahead and take a look. I'll wait."

He'd seen the message alert flashing out of the corner of his eye and it only took a moment for him to scroll through to the screen to open it. It was being recorded off a body-cam of some kind, probably concealed given the way edges of a jacket or shirt kept blocking the corner of the frame. The scenery was generic, green trees and dirt road. It could have come from almost anywhere. The house though...

He knew the house. He knew every peeling strip of white

paint, every crack in the windows of the old house. He'd spent his childhood on that back porch, throwing sticks for the dog to fetch, helping to tan leather from the deer he'd killed. His mother was sitting on the porch, not as she'd been when he was a child but as she was now, hair white and stringy, face cracked and older than her years. She was sewing something. She was always sewing something, fixing some clothes for herself or others who'd pay her in food or trade.

"I have finished cutting the firewood, Mrs. Patterson," the voice behind the camera announced with just the slightest hint of an accent. It could have come from anywhere in eastern Europe, but he'd learned it was Ukrainian. "Is there anything else you'd like me to do?"

"Naw, Lex, you've done enough for today." Cold fingers squeezed Patty's chest at the voice he hadn't heard in months now. "Honestly, I could find more stuff for you, but there's no more money left to pay you today."

"That's all right, ma'am," Lex replied, laughing. "I'll see you tomorrow then."

The body cam walked away from the house, back down the road to where a bicycle was leaning against a tree, saddlebags hanging from the seat. The camera stared into the left-hand bag as Lex pulled it open and the darkly polished lines of a Makarov automatic gleamed in the noonday sun for just a few seconds until Lex folded the flap back down.

"No!" Patty exclaimed involuntarily before realizing the video had ended.

"Don't worry, Geoffrey," Svetlana assured him, her voice coming from the phone's speaker loud enough for him to make it out even before he put the instrument back up to his ear. "Nothing has to happen to your mother, or your dear, sweet sister...or your little niece. As long as you do what you know must be done."

Patty's shoulders sagged, the air going out of him along with the will to fight. She owned him now, and she knew it.

"What do you want me to do?"

CHAPTER TWELVE_

NATE DECIDED to check the sat-com one last time before he went to bed. Wishful thinking maybe, hoping against hope the answers he waited for would be sitting there and not wanting to take the chance of letting them sit all night without seeing them. They seemed nebulous, prone to fading into the aether while no one watched, and he'd already cruised by the device four times just that day, despite resolving he wasn't going to do it again.

The light was on in the garage, the unfiltered yellow glow of the portable lanterns crawling out into the corridor beneath the swinging doors. He slowed his pace and checked his watch. It was well past one in the morning, 0100 he would have said if he'd still been in the Army or if he'd felt obligated to still use the terminology long after it ceased to have any real meaning. He had his Glock holstered at his waist; he'd been wearing it since the surprise attack, mostly because it gave him a feeling of security. A false one, most likely, since the 9mm wouldn't do shit against a Tagan, but he pulled it out anyway as he approached the door. This place was pretty remote and the likelihood of a squatter camping out here after all these years wasn't high, but he didn't want to get caught napping because he'd trusted in the odds.

He pushed the door open quickly, knowing it was going to squeak like a banshee on crack and wanting to get through before anyone had time to target it. Shadows drew his eye with flickers of darkness in his peripheral vision and he whipped the barrel of the Glock back and forth from one phantom target to another before he realized he was alone. Trying to relax, trying to get his breathing back under control, he shoved the automatic into its holster and walked across the stained cement floor with affected casualness, as if he hadn't nearly put a bullet into the shadow of a toolbox.

The sat-com was still hooked up. He hadn't taken it apart again after the second time he'd checked it, so that was no surprise. It was also powered up, which *was* a surprise. It ran off a rechargeable battery and he shut it off after each use to preserve the charge as long as possible before he had to hook it up to the solar generator.

Maybe Roach snuck in here earlier tonight to see if there was a reply yet.

The blinking red light on the corner of the screen stopped him in his tracks. There was a message. They'd sent a reply already...but if Roach had seen it, why hadn't she come and got him?

He hit a key to turn the screen on and the text popped up immediately, followed by a compressed image of a map.

POSSIBLE LOCATION OF RUSSIAN BASE OF OPERA-TIONS DETERMINED VIA SATELLITE SCAN, the text read. SEE FOLLOWING COORDINATES AND ATTACHED MAP. ACT ON YOUR OWN DISCRETION.

He checked the coordinates, frowning at the nagging thought they looked familiar. Then he scrolled down to bring the map up to fill the screen. It was an old map, pre-war but with all the modern sector designations stamped over the old names. Williamsburg. Yorktown. There was no mistaking the area highlighted as the target, though, across the river past the navy yards. A snort of dark amusement escaped him against his will.

Busch Gardens. The Russians were set up in Busch fucking Gardens.

Urgency surged inside him, a conviction they couldn't wait for reinforcements. He had to get everyone moving on this immediately, get to the Russians before they had time to plan another ambush or surprise attack, before they lost anyone else. He turned to head back into the offices, intent on rousing them from their sleep and getting them geared up…and then he noticed it.

Had they still been back at the warehouse, it would have jumped out at him immediately because he was used to the arrangement there, knew where everyone's private corner was, knew where their mechs were set up. Here, the absence gnawed at him unnoticed until he stared right at it. Four Hellfires stood watch from the rear wall of the garage in their maintenance cages, with one metal framework conspicuously unoccupied. Patty's. It was Patty's mech missing.

Where it had stood, a note was affixed to the wall, a small, yellow square from one of the office notepads they'd found all over the place. Nate ripped it away and brought it closer to the light to read it.

SAW THE MESSAGE ABOUT THE RUSSIANS. THIS IS MY FAULT, DIX IS DEAD BECAUSE OF ME. I'M GOING TO TAKE CARE OF THEM MYSELF. THE REST OF YOU SHOULDN'T HAVE TO GET HURT BECAUSE OF ME.

"Oh, Goddammit, Patty!" he exploded. He turned and sprinted through the door, heading for Roach and Ramirez. "Mata!" he bellowed ahead of him. "Roach! Wake the hell up!"

Patty let go of the handholds at the bottom of his Hellfire's cockpit and dropped to the pavement, bending his knees to absorb the impact. He'd done it a thousand times, but this time he lost his balance and had to catch himself against the leg of the machine. His knees felt weak, his hands trembled and his stomach was clenching as if he were about to go over a drop on one of the ancient rollercoasters he'd seen on the way in. Their tracks were Roman roads, monuments left over from another time.

Svetlana waited for him just a few meters from where he'd landed the Hellfire, as starkly, dangerously beautiful as ever, yet he barely spared her a glance. Three Tagans loomed above her, their running lights blinding him whenever he tried to look up at them, and yet they drew his eyes inexorably. Their chain guns weren't *quite* pointed directly at him, but close enough for him to move very slowly.

"I'm gratified you showed up, Geoffrey," she said, smiling as warmly as if she didn't have forty tons of metal for backup. "I had begun to worry."

"You made it pretty clear what would happen if I didn't," he said. He'd meant it to sound angry, bitter, but instead, his tone was petulant, a little fearful in his own ears. "I need you to get your damned goons away from my mother."

"Your mother will be fine," she assured him, moving closer, her hand resting on his chest. "As long as you keep the bargain you've agreed to and don't do anything stupid...like trying to run out on us."

"I'm here," he ground out, not feeling the least bit enticed by the woman. "I did what you said. They should be coming after me..." He shrugged. "...if they're going to bother."

"Of course they will bother, Geoffrey." Her tone was scolding, as if he were a wayward child who'd said something ridiculous. "You stole several million dollars' worth of pi-mech and weaponry. They'll want it back."

"They don't deserve to die because of me." The words were hollow, worthless. She was going to do what she was going to do and he didn't matter a damn to her. That much had become clear to him.

Dumb Kentucky hick, that's all I am to her. Maybe that's all I am to anyone.

"Nobody has to die," she said, her expression infuriatingly cheerful.

"You keep saying that," he snapped, anger finally overcoming fear, if only for a moment. He tried to push forward, but found, to his amazement, he couldn't move past the pressure of her hand on his chest. She was much stronger than she looked. "But you haven't given them the choice to do anything but fight. Why not offer *them* money? Why not give them the chance you gave me?"

"Because, my dear Geoffrey, they wouldn't take it." She cocked her head at him, still the teacher with the slow child who wouldn't learn his lesson. "You've lived with them for months now, yet you haven't come to know them at least this much? Nathan Stout is a true believer in the American dream, even though it's been dead for twice as long as he's been alive. Rachel Mata is a military brat. Her father was a Marine and she would never dishonor his memory by turning traitor. And Hector Ramirez..." She sniffed. "He'd be too scared. He doesn't have any family, has no home to go back to. If he were to lose this, he would have nothing."

She let her hand slip away and began circling him, a cat playing with a mouse.

"But you, Geoffrey Alan Patterson from Frankfort, Kentucky, the fetid, unwashed navel of this smoldering, radioactive wreck of a country, you have it all. You have a home, a family waiting for you, depending on you for survival. You have no ties to the military, no illusions of patriotism or honor, no allegiance to this country or any other. People in Appalachia take care of themselves or they die? Isn't that right?"

Her breath was a knife caressing the back of his neck and he shuddered, stepping away from her but freezing when the stance of one of the Tagans shifted just slightly, the muzzle of its anti-personnel machine gun moving ever so slightly.

"That's the way it is," he agreed, jaws clenching on what he wanted to say, on the names he wanted to call her.

Psycho Russian bitch.

"Who better to offer the money he so desperately needs, then? Do you think I don't know my job?" Her forefinger jabbed into his upper arm for emphasis and he flinched. "Do you think I was sent here to this shithole simply because I was expendable?"

"The thought had crossed my mind," he admitted maliciously. "I mean, this ain't exactly a premium assignment for a KGB agent."

"I asked to come here." Now she seemed genuinely pissed off, which was scary but also something of a minor triumph. It was hard to get a rise out of the woman, except in bed, and she could have been faking that. *Probably was faking that,* he admitted to himself.

"I volunteered because I was needed," she went on, circling back around in front of him. "Because there's something bigger at stake than who controls this God-forsaken swamp. And it's important enough to pay an unskilled, uneducated, desperate redneck hillbilly like you a million adjusted dollars, and more than important enough to kill you and your whole worthless family if it comes to it. It's so close to the end, Geoff. Just play your part." She smiled and leaned up, kissing him with such fierce passion he almost thought it was real…until he realized it was simply a demonstration of how good she was at her job. "Maybe," she said breathlessly, "you'll even live through this."

Patty watched the sky through his Hellfire's canopy. It was a reflexive action—he could have just looked straight ahead at the threat display and seen thermal, infrared and visual all melded seamlessly into one, coherent picture of his surroundings. But he'd seen them coming in on radar and he knew where to look. The night was clear, the moon sinking in the early morning hours, and three stars shone in the sky from the thrusters burning in.

He was glad it was dark. This place was depressing in the daytime, the fake nature it had once sold now overgrown with the real thing. Buildings had collapsed under the weight of the years and the ones still standing were stained and mottled and peeling. Rollercoaster tracks twisted and spiraled and soared and dove, motionless and rusted. It was a tombstone for a way of life he'd never get to experience. The whole region was a cemetery infested with people too stupid to know they were dead.

Just like the three people landing their Hellfires in front of him now.

"Patty, what the hell do you think you're doing?" Roach bellowed, her voice so loud over his cockpit speakers that they exploded in static. He could tell which mech was hers even without the IFF transponder because it took a step toward him, breaking the line with the other two, its articulated hand cocked as if to throw a punch.

He'd expected her to lose her shit. It was Nate's place to chew him out, but she was bossy, couldn't bear anyone else getting a word in edgewise. That made it easier.

"I was being stupid," he admitted, trying to put some truth in with the lie to make it more convincing. "I felt guilty about Dix so I thought I'd try to end this myself, but I can't. There are three of them in Tagans and I can't take that many on myself."

"Where are they?" Nate asked him. He could hear the strain in the man's voice; Nate was angry, but keeping it under control for the good of the mission. That was Nate, always under control, always holding everything in check. He wondered if the guy ever got laid.

Ramirez said nothing, and Patty figured the Mule was sweating bullets, scared shitless to be out here with just them.

"Over in the France section of the park," he told them. He wouldn't have had any idea what "France" was if Svetlana hadn't told him, but he had to make it look like he'd scoped the place out. "It's over to the north of..."

"I know where it is," Nate interrupted him.

"Yeah, well, the Russian mechs are set up behind this tall stage at the Royal Palace amphitheater, and I think their base of operations is either inside that building or maybe underground. I think there are tunnels underneath the buildings."

"You've seen Russians going in and out of the building?" Roach asked him, still sounding angry but also curious.

She turned her armor toward the direction he'd indicated. Nate didn't, but he was experienced, real military. She was just a wannabe with daddy issues.

And what does that make me? Oh yeah...desperate.

"I saw someone poke their head out," he answered her question. "I was too far away to catch an accent. Hopefully far enough away he didn't see me or my mech."

"All right, here's what we'll do," Nate said. "Roach, you and Mule fly around the other side of the park, come in from the north down into the amphitheater. Make a big show of it, get their attention. Patty, you and I will give them a minute to get into position, then we'll come in low, between the buildings and take the bad guys from the rear while they're distracted. Hit 'em fast, hit 'em hard and hit 'em again before they realize what's happening. Should be simple, hooah?"

Patty rolled his eyes. "Hooah" was an Army thing, an all-purpose exclamation they used to show how hyped up they were to do something tedious or stupid or dangerous. Still, he was trying to sell this, so...

"Hooah," he chimed in with the others.

"Get going, Roach."

"Understood, Boss," Roach said, which seemed a little odd to Patty but she was an odd chick.

Roach and the Mule blasted away from them on gouts of wavering, glowing fire, curving off slightly to the left to get around the coaster tracks looming above them. Patty's stomach churned as he watched them go, knowing he was sending them into a trap, hoping it wasn't to their death. But better theirs than his...or his mom's. Less than a year ago, these people had been strangers to him. He kept trying to remind himself of that.

"Just you and me now, Patty," Nate said. There was a strange note to his voice, something almost regretful. "Time to be honest."

He felt a prickling up the back of his neck, a sense something wasn't right. He might have ignored it, might have tried to play it off, but not now, not with what was happening. He knew he had one chance, one clean shot while Nate wasn't expecting it...

His cockpit went suddenly and irrevocably dark, the instruments going dead, his Hellfire freezing in place with a gently fading hum of servos, not even audible until they stopped working. Patty's breath caught in his chest and a cold numbness spread outward from his gut as he realized what was happening.

"How did you know?" he asked, not even sure if his question would leave the cockpit with the power out. "How did you do it?"

The radio crackled in his headset, the only thing in the cockpit still live.

"I'm too trusting sometimes, Patty," Nate said. "Dix wasn't. He built a remote cut-off for all our mechs. Don't bother trying to get out the hatch, either. The lock is sealed and the emergency canopy ejection is disabled. As for how I knew...you're way too young to have ever been here, to have even heard of this place. How the hell would you know which part was the France pavilion? Shit, they're aren't even any signs left up. Why did you do it, Patty? *How* could you do it to us...to Dix?"

That hurt, a literal, physical pain in his chest and he pounded his fist into the armrest of his seat.

"For my family, man," he moaned. "They know where my mom is...they have a guy there. They sent me video."

"And before that, it was the money, wasn't it? You sold us out for money."

"You know why I need it, Nate," he insisted. He hated the words, hated how they made him sound. "What are you going to do?"

There was a long pause and Patty wasn't sure the man would bother to answer. When he did, the sadness remained.

"Right now, I'm going to go kill your Russian friends. After that...well, I'll decide how much more killing I feel like doing."

There was a roar of jets and Nate was gone. Patty slumped in his seat and waited, alone, in the dark, to see who would eventually win, to see which of his friends would wind up killing him.

CHAPTER THIRTEEN_

Nate couldn't understand why he wasn't enraged. He should have been seething, murderous, ready to kill the damned Russians and then go back and beat Geoff Patterson to death with his bare hands, but he was just...numb. He flew the Hellfire in a curve around the roller coaster track with the rote motions of a trained pilot, checking his weapons and sensor with the flat, emotionless precision of a professional pilot.

Just as well. Giving in to the anger would just get me killed. There's work to do.

"Roach, Mule, you read?"

"We're here, Boss," Roach told him. *She* was pissed and not trying to hide it. But she'd had time to prepare because, unlike what he'd told Patty, he'd suspected what was going on the moment he'd seen the note. Patty was many things, one of them being a very competent mech pilot, but Nate had known there was no way in hell Patty would take off after the Russians on his own. Patty fought for Patty.

So, when they'd flown into Busch Gardens, Nate had been looking for an ambush. He'd found it at the amphitheater at the France pavilion, spotted it from behind the trees. There were, indeed, three Tagans standing beside the stage of the old Royal Palace amphitheater, but they were U-mechs, uncrewed, remotely piloted. He wouldn't have been able to tell without the data Dix had retrieved after the ambush at the old navy yards, but now he could spot the tell-tale signal from the communications system sent back to the Pi-mechs controlling the drones. These weren't being flown by someone in a van with a joystick and a satellite uplink, they were mirroring Pi-mechs, which meant there were three *more* Tagans prepped and ready to jump them when they went after the drones.

There were only so many places you could hide a ten-meter-tall anthropomorphic tank and the only one nearby was in the Germany pavilion, behind what had once, many decades ago, been the Curse of DarKastle ride. He was only aware of it from a stray memory from his Prime of a visit squeezed in between training sessions, of his disappointment that the ride wasn't open. It had been closed once before in 2018, then reopened many years later, larger and revamped and had revitalized the place for a while, until things fell apart.

It remained the largest structure in the park, a crumbling, rotting façade of a medieval castle. Crenellations had been smoothed out by the ravages of time and weather and at least one fire, and what had once been the central tower had fallen years ago, but the exterior walls still stood...and behind them, he was fairly certain, were three Tagans.

They were going to do just what he'd suggested to Patty, but he was going to be the bait while Roach and Mule sprung the trap. Two-to-one were long odds, but all they had to do was take out the manned mechs and the drones would go inactive. Unless they had a satellite back-up, but even then, it would take time for the control to switch and they could take the U-Mechs out during the delay.

That's the plan, anyway.

He swooped down around the front of the Royal Theater, staying low, just above where the plastic seats had waited for the next kitschy act to come on stage. The seats were mostly gone as well, either stolen or broken or melted, and the floor of the amphitheater was littered with garbage and debris almost a meter thick. His jets kicked up roiling sprays of dried grass, paper, plastic and the accumulated filth of decades of neglect as he passed low over the floor, pretending to be stealthy.

Something darted away, hot and fast on thermal, but he was fairly sure it was a coyote. He reached the end of the stage and swung around it and there they were, glowing hot, their isotope reactors North Stars in the depth of the night. They were bunched together far too close, moving far too slow to be anything but a trap, but he had to make this look good.

He cut loose with the twin 40mms on his left shoulder, the cannons pounding like jackhammers beside his cockpit, strafing across the three Tagans as he flew past them and touched down just behind the stage. The rounds were signal flares in the darkness, streaks of fire terminating in glowing spheres of destruction; and by their light, he could see the Tagans rocking back under the impacts. He'd switched his load out from the standard frag to vehicle interdiction rounds, still probably not enough to penetrate the heavy armor on the vitals of the Tagans, but better than harsh language.

The U-mechs reacted slowly, ponderously, like men who'd been punched in the face and had to shake it off before fighting back. Nate thought it might be a result of the operators' indecision on whether to spring the ambush on just one Hellfire when they'd expected three, but he wasn't going to write a letter of complaint about it. He touched down lightly, lithely on the cracked and stained concrete of the stage, breaking into a sprint the second the mech's footpads gained purchase.

The Tagans were spinning, lifting slowly away on

screaming jets of fire, but he was inside their direction of turn, one step ahead of the firing arc for their cannons and too close for them to use missiles. He kept pounding them with the 40mms, one round after another from almost point-blank range, just hoping he'd get lucky and hit something vulnerable and, for once in his short life, he got lucky.

The Tagan furthest from him was simultaneously trying to turn and ascend on its thrusters in an awkward movement, like a great blue heron startled from its perch taking flight. The motion exposed its back to Nate and it was too sweet a target to pass up. He'd been saving his primary weapons for the real enemy, but he toggled over to his Vulcan with instincts too deeply ingrained to fight and put a two-second burst into the U-mech's thruster cowling.

The vectored thrust nozzle ruptured with a shower of sparks and flame and the jet exhaust burst through the thin veneer of what was left, sending the U-mech careening off to Nates left and smashing into the auditorium floor with a thunderous crunch of metal Nate could hear even through the cockpit fuselage. Smoke billowed up around the wrecked machine glowing with the flames pouring out of its thrusters and that, he thought with grim satisfaction, was strike one.

He couldn't let the others get him in their firing arc, couldn't afford to allow the controllers in the Pi-mechs to have an instant to strategize. He hit his thrusters and grabbed the closest of the drones by the arm, using his leverage and the power of his thrusters to yank the Tagan between his Hellfire and the last of the drones, using it as a shield just as the third machine finally opened fire with its chain gun.

25mm rounds pummeled the Tagan, pushing it against his Hellfire and knocking them both backward, just a short burst before the pilot remotely controlling the U-mech let his finger off the trigger, but it was enough to disable the drone he'd grabbed hold of.

Strike two.

He kept hold of the smoldering wreckage of the drone and leapt forward, the thrust of his mech's jets carrying him and fifteen tons of limp metal just far enough to slam it into the chest of the remaining Tagan. Nate let the dead husk of the drone go and his thrusters carried him upward, directly over the top of the last enemy U-mech. He swiveled his 40mm's downward and emptied what was left of the cannon's twin magazines straight into the vulnerable cockpit canopy of the drone. There was no human inside for the rounds to kill, but enough of the blast made its way through the narrow polymer canopy to disable the communications gear and the drone immediately settled back to a gentle landing and froze in place, waiting patiently for someone to come repair it.

"Strike three, fuckers," he said aloud, transmitted on an open frequency. "Who's next up to bat?"

"You are a very good pilot, Captain Stout."

He blinked. He hadn't been expecting an answer. The voice was smooth and deep and intoxicating, like fine, aged whiskey, not sounding very much like a Russian mech pilot.

"But as a good pilot," she went on, "you should know when the odds are against you."

There they were, three Tagans, naked and glowing on radar and thermal, jetting out from behind the remains of the make-believe castle and spreading out with the smooth precision of real, human pilots, men and women who wore the mech like a suit, felt its limbs move as if they were their own.

"As a good pilot," Nate responded, bringing his Hellfire slowly up on its thrusters to meet them. "I know never to take on heavy odds without backup."

There was a warbling, ululating shout, what he guessed was

Roach's best imitation of a rebel yell, and the two Hellfires shot out on glowing jets of fire, rising above the remains of the old train station and splitting up to each take one of the Tagans. Nate bared his teeth in an unseen challenge and headed for the Russian mech at the center of the three-pronged formation, firing off two Mark-Ex missiles, one after another. The twin launches rocked his Hellfire back in its flight, pushing roughly, violently with the force of their solid fuel rockets igniting.

This was why he'd saved the weapons, why he'd used the forties against the U-mechs. This was the real fight. He followed the missiles in, trailing behind their twenty-gravity acceleration with something more sedate, toggling his joystick trigger to the 20mm cannon.

The Tagan tried evasive maneuvers, breaking low and skirting back around the walls of the castle, dogged by the Mark-Ex missiles, and all of them disappeared from view behind the huge building. Nate arced over the roof, noticing the heat warning on his thrusters and knowing he'd have to put down soon. Before he'd made it across the sagging, cracked surface of the roof, twin blasts echoed through the night, lighting up the other side of the castle with the crackling, popping flashes of several kilograms of high-explosive warheads igniting.

Nate hoped the missiles had taken the Russian out, but he wasn't going to count on it. He dropped down into the midst of the rising clouds of smoke and dust from the explosions, cutting his jets early to avoid hanging in mid-air and making too big of a target. His Hellfire landed hard, the knees and hips bending to absorb the impact, but the force of it still enough to clack his teeth together inside his helmet.

His jaw was going to be sore, but it could have been worse—two rounds of 25mm passed just half a meter over the top of his mech and blew a man-sized hole through the exterior wall of the castle, clouds of plaster dust and smoke joining the mist from the missile blasts. Nate was moving immediately, instinctively, before the location of the Tagan even registered with his conscious mind, before he could interpret the data from the thermal sensors and lidar in his threat display.

The Tagan was only fifteen meters away, kneeling in the splintered wreckage of a scrawny tree planted for landscaping decades ago yet still undersized from lack of water and sunlight. The Russian mech had put it out of its misery, smashing into it in his quest to avoid the missiles, and he was halfway back to his feet, crouching like a Revolutionary War soldier reloading his musket while the next line took their shot.

Nate knew what *he* would do, and he had to assume the Tagan's pilot was at least as well-trained and disciplined, whether it was true or not. He came out of the landing with a powerful spring of the Hellfire's legs boosted by a brief firing of the thrusters and lunged forward and to the right of the Tagan just as the Russian mech launched its own missile. At point-blank range, there would have been no time for evasion or anti-missile machine gun fire; he would have been dead instantly.

Instead, the Russian version of the Mark-Ex, the MJK-38F, soared off into the night blindly, too close and fired too quickly for a laser-lock, destined to spend itself kilometers away, hopefully not into the house of some poor squatter. Nate wasn't as worried about collateral damage from the first enemy missile as he was about where the next one might go.

He circled the Tagan, galloping the Hellfire in a tight curl away from the arc of fire of the Russian's chain gun. The 25mm chattered spitefully, the rounds passing just behind him as they raced for the tipping point, the spot where one or the other would be forced to take to the air and would, in that instant, give the other a shot. The Tagan pilot was good, but he was also human and just as given to the fears of any soldier. He'd seen Nate take down three U-mechs by himself and some small, nagging voice inside his head had to be telling him he was in trouble.

The Russian blinked. It didn't take much to hit the thrusters, just a stomp of a foot pedal, but the motion arrested his spin, stopped the arc of his main gun and the threat it presented. Nate skidded to a halt, his 20mm tracking upward, his finger tightening on the trigger. There was just a space of second where the Tagan was vulnerable, but a second was ten rounds of tungsten-core 20mm. The burst caught the Tagan just under its right arm, spearing through the torso and through the pilot inside.

The jets cut off abruptly with the loss of a pressure on the throttle, and the massive Tagan collapsed like a felled tree, crashing into the pavement with a traffic-accident cacophony of rending metal. The Tagan wasn't dead, wasn't disabled, but it lay motionless, waiting for commands from its master.

Nate risked a flash of the floodlight on his Hellfire's chest and saw a red mist against the clear polymer of the Tagan's canopy, all that was left of the pilot. Should he have felt bad for the man? Should he have felt guilty for ending another human life? The man might have been a draftee, with as little choice in coming here as Nate had been given for his very existence.

Fuck it. If he didn't want me to kill him, he should have been a better pilot.

Nate hit the jets and climbed up to the mech's hundred-meter ceiling, spinning in place, trying to get a reading on where the others had gone. IFF signals beeped data at him, showing him Roach two kilometers to his north, on the ground but moving, the thermal signature of a Tagan running just ahead of her. She was always the hunter, never the hunted. Dix had told Nate he thought she'd wind up a better pilot than either of them with enough experience.

Ramirez, on the other hand...the boy was flying, and from

the heat readings off his mech, he'd been flying too long, was close to heat shutdown, but he was dodging erratically, running scared. The Russian mech on his tail was three hundred meters back, wasting a burst from his 25mm every few seconds to try to nudge Ramirez's course into his missile targeting reticle. It was working—Ramirez's dodges and weaves were narrowing and he didn't have much time left before one of those unimaginatively-named Russian air-to-air birds went right up his ass.

Lucky for him I saved a couple missiles of my own.

It took about three seconds to get a targeting lock on the Tagan, enough time for Ramirez to take a grazing hit from a 25mm round—Nate could see the sparks from hundreds of meters away, felt a stab of urgency and considered jetting in to distract the Russian, but the thought was interrupted by a good tone and a green reticle. He hit the launch control twice, felt the Hellfire lurch in mid-air as the missiles streaked away from it.

"Mule!" he called to Ramirez. "Break right and get to the ground!"

Before your turbines overheat and you crash, he didn't say because there was no point in panicking the kid any more than he already was.

The missiles curled in to track the Tagan and he'd seen them coming because he climbed sharply and headed for the nearest cover, a roller coaster track. The Russian just made it over the tracks before the missiles hit, both of them slamming into a looped section and wasting their warheads on twisted, rusted metal.

"Shit," Nate said mildly. Mark-Ex missiles weren't cheap and he'd just blown two of them on public vandalism.

The looped section of coaster track shuddered and swayed and finally, broke off and tumbled to the pavement below. The Tagan shot out from beneath it just before it hit, and a cloud of dirt and dust climbed up to join the smoke from the missile explosions. Ramirez had landed near the river running through the center of the park and ducked beneath the trees; Nate could still see his thermal signature, but it would be hard for the Tagan to get missile lock on him with so much foliage in the way.

Targeting Nate wouldn't be nearly as difficult. The Russian mech fired on him the second it was clear of the roller coaster tracks, two of the MJK-38F missiles flaring away from the launch tubes affixed to the Tagan's right shoulder.

That missile needs a nickname. Back in the old days, we used to give Russian weapons systems and fighter planes stupid-sounding nicknames like Flogger and Foxbat. This one should be called the Fruit-fly, maybe, or the Brickbat. Yeah, Brickbat, I like that.

Nate didn't try to outrun the newly-christened Brickbats, they were too close for him to make it more than a hundred meters and there was no convenient cover he could reach in time. Instead, he set down on the pavement and let the Hellfire's anti-missile defense have a go at them, standing still to make it easier for the radar to track them.

It was hard, standing in the open instead of bolting, but that was part of being an experienced pilot, knowing when to run and knowing when to stand. The 6.5mm machine guns on either side of the Hellfire's torso chattered rhythmically, guided by computer targeting, by a series of 1's and 0's programmed somewhere down the line by a human typing them into an input terminal probably a decade ago.

Whoever that was, they just saved my life.

The warheads flamed out within a half-second of each other, what was left of the rocket motors tumbling out of control in fireworks-show sprays of flaming propellant, but Nate didn't bother watching them fall. He was already moving, knowing the Tagan would be using the time to close in on him. The pilot had struck him as older, patient, perhaps a bit too patient. He could have taken Ramirez out by taking more of a chance, but instead, he'd sat back and tried to nudge him into an easy kill.

Older pilot, been at this a while, not eager to get himself killed. Have to use that.

Nate hit the thrusters and flew straight at the Tagan, not trying to get fancy with some elaborate flanking maneuver. The Russian wouldn't want a head-on confrontation, Nate could feel it in his gut, so it was no surprise when the Tagan jetted off in a wide parabola away from the Hellfire, heading for the old parking lots.

He's been up for over three minutes now, closer to four. He'll be near the redline, have to set that thing down or risk a shutdown. And he doesn't like risk.

He went down right on schedule, not into the middle of the parking lot because that would have put him too far into the open. Instead, he touched ground behind a stand of trees and brush, once well-tended and decorative but now gone wild and overgrown.

Trying to throw off my missile targeting. Not that I have any missiles left, but he doesn't know that. He's going to sit back there and wait for me to come around either side of the trees, where he can get a clean shot at me.

But the Russian didn't know his trees. These were silver maples. Nate wasn't sure why the Prime had known this, or why the techs who'd programmed his brain with selected portions of the Prime's memory had considered it important data to pass on, but he recognized the trees for what they were. It was fast-growing, landscape ready, favored by the sort of businesses who would have planted decorative trees in the park.

It was also weak and brittle.

Nate came in low, only a meter off the ground, and plowed his Hellfire right through the trunk of the center tree, blasting it to splinters and sending an explosion of bark and leaves and moss flying out the other side. He came out nearly on top of the enemy mech, much too close for the Russian pilot to react in time.

He'd already had his 20mm lined up with the Tagan and all it took was a squeeze on the trigger. 20mm tungsten slugs chewed through the Russian mech's cockpit, impossible to miss at this range. The Tagan had been in the middle of a step and without the guidance of its pilot, it toppled backward, cracking the pavement where it hit.

Nate pulled in a deep breath, starting to feel the adrenalin shakes now that the deed was done.

"Roach," he called. "Do you need help?"

"What do you think?" The reply was harsh, sarcastic. She wasn't in a good mood, and he didn't blame her. "The Gomer is down and I'm fine. What's our next move?"

"Meet me back where I left Patty," he said grimly. "Bring Ramirez."

This, he was beginning to realize, would be the hard part.

CHAPTER FOURTEEN_

The melancholy glint of false dawn teased at the eastern horizon by the time they made it back to Patty. He was right where they'd left him.

Nate had half hoped the man might somehow have gotten free of the cockpit and ran, that he wouldn't ever see him again, wouldn't be forced to make the decision he was about to make. But Patty was still slumped in his seat, surrendered to the inevitable. Was he just stupid and lazy, Nate wondered, or did he feel so guilty he hadn't even tried?

Nate shut down his Hellfire slowly, methodically, absorbing himself in the routine and trying not to think. He noted every reading, marking it down on his log as if he were on a training run. Winchester on missiles, 6.5mm machine gun and 40mm cannon ammunition. Twenty-three rounds of 20mm remaining. Various minor damage, only pressing matter was a hip actuator close to failing. He'd have to get that looked at.

Good thing they didn't bring any more Tagans. We'd have been fucked.

Then there were no more excuses and no time left to waste. He sighed deeply and yanked loose his seat harness, pulling off his helmet and hanging it from the armrest of his chair. The lower hatch opened with the kick of a lever and he slowly and carefully climbed downward out of the Hellfire, toeing the retractable stepladder down rather than dropping the last two meters. There was no hurry.

Ramirez and Roach were already out of their mechs, waiting for him with obvious impatience.

They're young. Young people are always impatient, even for the bad times. Get them over with and get past them, they figure. They don't understand how the bad times shape you, change you in ways you don't want to change. If they knew, they wouldn't rush into them.

Nate pulled his Glock from its chest holster and nodded to Ramirez.

"Get him out."

Ramirez made a face, as if he wanted to complain about still being the Mule, having to do the shit jobs. Nate checked the load on his 9mm and didn't bother to look at Ramirez.

"Watch him, Roach," he said. "Don't let him try to grab Ramirez."

Rachel Mata slid a broad-bladed knife from her belt and snarled an acknowledgement.

"I hope the fucker resists."

Patty might have been a dumb-assed hillbilly, but he was smarter than that. Once Ramirez unlocked his hatch and pulled it open, Patty climbed down slowly and without making any sudden moves.

"Why the fuck would you do it?" Ramirez demanded.

"Forget it," Nate snapped before Patty could even think about replying. "I already know why he did it. That's not the question. The question is, what are we going to do about him?"

"We could turn him over to the Department of Defense liaison," Ramirez suggested, the trusting naivete in his expression almost enough to make Nate laugh. "They could get him to the CIA, maybe."

Patty's head came up at that, eyes going to Nate almost as if he was curious if the man would shove the decision upstairs, avoid the responsibility.

"DoD policy," Nate said, "is that every military contractor handles their own discipline. They don't have the people or the time to be prosecuting all the shitbags who pass through the training."

"But this is treason, Nate," Roach objected, eyes widening. "He sold us out to the enemy. Surely they'd want to…"

"It's my call, Rachel." His voice was flat, a gavel on a bench. "I'm the one who's responsible for every one of you and everything you do while you're under contract with me."

"What are you going to do?" Patty asked. He hadn't spoken till now, just stood watching in stoic silence, as if he'd accepted his fate. Even this question wasn't plaintive or fearful, just curious.

Nate stared at him, wondering if he kept staring long enough, whether the truth might leap out at him and save him from what he knew he had to do.

"Roach, Mule," he said, eyes still locked on Patty's, "get back in your mechs and head back to base."

"What?" Ramirez blurted. "Why?"

"Because I fucking said so."

"Nate, you don't have to do this alone," Roach said, taking a step toward him.

"Yes, I do," he interrupted, stopping her advance with an upraised palm. "Get back in your Hellfire and get out of here now. That's an order."

She stood her ground, eyes boring into him. He could feel them, but he refused to meet them. Finally, she cursed and turned away, sliding her knife back into its sheath.

"Fuck you, man," she muttered as she pulled herself back up into her mech. Nate wasn't sure if the words were aimed at him or Patty, or maybe both.

He didn't say another word until after he heard the Hellfires' turbines wailing to life, felt the hot blast of their thrusters as they lifted away. The Glock had been held at low ready, but now he raised it to aim directly at Patty's chest.

"You really gonna do it, man?" Patty asked him. It was almost a dare. "You really going to kill me?"

"It feels like I kill people every day," Nate said, almost whispering, not even sure if he was talking to Patty. He raised his voice to make sure the other man heard him. "I just killed two men a few minutes ago. Your Russian buddies. Does that make you sad?"

"Whoever won, I was going to wind up dead. These guys don't put up with people failing." Patty squeezed his eyes shut for a second, as if it was all finally catching up to him. "Can you try to make sure they don't hurt my mom?"

Fuck.

"Fuck," he repeated aloud, lowering the gun from Patty's chest almost involuntarily before raising it back up again. He snarled, left hand balling into a fist, feeling like punching the other man. "Goddammit, Patty, why'd you have to do this? Why'd you put me in this fucking position?"

"I'm sorry, Nate." And it seemed as if he really was. There was genuine pain on his long, country face. "They get you a little at a time and by the time you figure out what's really going on, it's too late and there's no way out."

"Shit." Nate closed his eyes and let the gun fall to his side. "Shit, Patty, I can't do it. Just go, man."

He opened his eyes again and saw horror on Patty's face, the man's eyes wide and staring at something behind him. Nate spun, bringing the Glock up, but something sharp and burning stabbed into his neck and suddenly he was on the ground, every muscle in his body seizing. Consciousness narrowed to a black-rimmed tunnel and he only noticed the electric current had ceased when he felt a hand prying the gun from his quivering hand.

"You've been a bad boy, Geoffrey."

The voice was the same one he'd heard on the radio earlier, smooth, husky, very female. She was tall, impossibly tall, or maybe that was just him lying flat on the ground with her towering above him. Her hair was blond and her face...familiar.

She was the same woman he'd seen with Patty in the Fry.

"You let them sniff you out," the woman accused. "Treachery, I would expect. You're a traitor, after all. Incompetence is unforgivable."

There was a gunshot, two, the rattle of brass cartridge casings clattering to the pavement, then the meaty thump of a body following them down. He couldn't see it, couldn't force himself to move, to turn over and look.

Was the girl alone? No, he could hear footsteps, see the pant legs of others, men, large men dressed roughly in combat boots and tactical pants.

"Get him up."

A different voice. Male. Rough, as if the vocal cords had been damaged at some point. And yet...also familiar, somehow.

"I have been waiting a long time for this moment, Nathan. It has cost me much in lives and treasure, but I know it's going to be worth it."

Hands grasped his arms and yanked him up none too gently, and he could see the man attached to them were not the gentle sort. Scarred, muscular, with the cold, hardened eyes of experienced killers. He didn't try to fight them, sensing it would cost him unnecessary pain and not accomplish a damned thing. One of them still held the taser they'd used on him and he cursed in sudden pain as he felt someone yank the darts from the back of his neck.

The man who'd spoken was dressed in surprisingly casual clothes, jeans and a flannel shirt. He was taller than Nate, with the face of someone who'd been chubby but lost weight perforce from illness or deprivation. His hair was long and coarse, pulled into a salt-and-pepper ponytail and the face...

It was older than he remembered, lined and creased and weathered, but he *did* remember it.

"Bob," Nate hissed, barely able to find the breath to speak. "But...you're dead."

"Indeed, I am," Robert Franklin, longtime friend of Nate's Prime, inventor of the mech, confirmed cheerfully. "And so are you, Nate." He grinned, a familiar grin, good-natured and mischievous and so very like Bob. "But nothing lasts forever."

THANK YOU FOR READING HELLFIRE_

We hope you enjoyed it as much as we enjoyed bringing it to you. We just wanted to take a moment to encourage you to review the book. Follow this link: Hellfire to be directed to the book's Amazon product page to leave your review.

Every review helps further the author's reach and, ultimately, helps them continue writing fantastic books for us all to enjoy.

You can also join our non-spam mailing list by visiting www.subscribepage.com/AethonReadersGroup and never miss out on future releases. You'll also receive three full books completely Free as our thanks to you.

Facebook

Instagram

Twitter

Website

Want to discuss our books with other readers and even the authors? Join our Discord server today and be a part of the Aethon community.

ALSO IN THE SERIES_

HELLFIRE
BRIMSTONE
APOCALYPSE

If you enjoyed Mech Force, you will love Wholesale Slaughter!

Start a new adventure today!